SUSANN

Ruskin Bond's first novel, *The Room on the Roof*, written when he was seventeen, won the John Llewellyn Rhys Memorial Prize in 1957. Since then he has written several novellas (including *Vagrants in the Valley*, *A Flight of Pigeons* and *Delhi Is Not Far*), essays, poems and children's books, many of which have been published by Penguin India. He has also written over 500 short stories and articles that have appeared in a number of magazines and anthologies. He received the Sahitya Akademi Award in 1993 and the Padma Shri in 1999.

Ruskin Bond was born in Kasauli, Himachal Pradesh, and grew up in Jamnagar, Dehradun, Delhi and Shimla. As a young man, he spent four years in the Channel Islands and London. He returned to India in 1955 and has never left the country since. He now lives in Landour, Mussoorie, with his adopted family.

ALSO BY RUSKIN BOND

Fiction
The Room on the Roof & Vagrants in the Valley
The Night Train at Deoli and Other Stories
Time Stops at Shamli and Other Stories
Our Trees Still Grow in Dehra
A Season of Ghosts
When Darkness Falls and Other Stories
A Flight of Pigeons
Delhi Is Not Far
A Face in the Dark and Other Hauntings
The Sensualist
A Handful of Nuts

Non-fiction
Rain in the Mountains
Scenes from a Writer's Life
The Lamp Is Lit
The Little Book of Comfort
Landour Days
Notes from a Small Room

Anthologies
Dust on the Mountain: Collected Stories
The Best of Ruskin Bond
Friends in Small Places
Indian Ghost Stories (ed.)
Indian Railway Stories (ed.)
Classical Indian Love Stories and Lyrics (ed.)
Tales of the Open Road
Ruskin Bond's Book of Nature
Ruskin Bond's Book of Humour
A Town Called Dehra
Classic Ruskin Bond

Poetry
Ruskin Bond's Book of Verse

Susanna's Seven Husbands

RUSKIN BOND

With a screenplay by
VISHAL BHARDWAJ *and* MATTHEW ROBBINS

"Durga"
This goes to you with good
wishes for your happiness
and success! Ruskin Bond
29/3/11

PENGUIN BOOKS

PENGUIN BOOKS

Published by the Penguin Group

Penguin Books India Pvt. Ltd, 11 Community Centre, Panchsheel Park, New Delhi 110 017, India

Penguin Group (USA) Inc., 375 Hudson Street, New York, New York 10014, USA

Penguin Group (Canada), 90 Eglinton Avenue East, Suite 700, Toronto, Ontario, M4P 2Y3, Canada (a division of Pearson Penguin Canada Inc.)

Penguin Books Ltd, 80 Strand, London WC2R 0RL, England

Penguin Ireland, 25 St Stephen's Green, Dublin 2, Ireland (a division of Penguin Books Ltd)

Penguin Group (Australia), 250 Camberwell Road, Camberwell, Victoria 3124, Australia (a division of Pearson Australia Group Pty Ltd)

Penguin Group (NZ), 67 Apollo Drive, Rosedale, North Shore 0632, New Zealand (a division of Pearson New Zealand Ltd)

Penguin Group (South Africa) (Pty) Ltd, 24 Sturdee Avenue, Rosebank, Johannesburg 2196, South Africa

Penguin Books Ltd, Registered Offices: 80 Strand, London WC2R 0RL, England

First published by Penguin Books India 2011

ISBN 9780143416111

Typeset in Sabon by InoSoft Systems, Noida
Printed at Thomson Press (I) Ltd.

contents

preface

I first met Vishal Bhardwaj when he bought the film rights to my story, 'The Blue Umbrella', which he made into a delightful film for picture-goers of all ages.

After that I did some writing for him, and at his suggestion developed my short story 'Susanna's Seven Husbands' into a novella, creating new characters and incidents. Vishal and Matthew Robbins based their screenplay on this version, and I thought it would be a good idea if we published the novella, short story and screenplay together, thus giving the reader an insight into the way a short story becomes a film story and then a screenplay! Ravi Singh of Penguin India encouraged the idea, and here's the result.

This was not the end of my involvement with 7 *Khoon Maaf*. Vishal suggested that I play a small role in the film, and I readily agreed, thus making my film debut at the age of seventy-six! I had two brief scenes with the beautiful and talented Priyanka Chopra, and I enjoyed the experience of working with her and the entire unit, on location in Pondicherry, and in Mumbai at a beautiful old church in Byculla.

7 *Khoon Maaf* is a very different film from *The Blue Umbrella*. All of Vishal's films are unique in their own way. I see him as the Hitchcock of Indian cinema, a master of the macabre. And with some sauce and spice added to the suspense!

RUSKIN BOND

introduction

I remember feeling amused and intrigued when I first came across the title 'Susanna's Seven Husbands' in a collection of Ruskin Bond's short stories that he had sent me. How and why would somebody get married seven times? Curious, I immediately began reading the story. The wacky side of Ruskin Bond unfolded slowly in front of my eyes. The character of Susanna captivated me, and I was amazed with Ruskin Saab's ability as a writer to sketch a character who was so interesting, wicked, but at the same time endearing.

The story stayed with me for a long time. I saw the possibility of a very unusual film in it but I didn't make any move to acquire the rights. A few months later a film-maker friend of mine called me to say that he was desperately looking for a story and asked whether I could help him find one. I sent him the tale of the seven murders committed by the beautiful Susanna, written in Ruskin Bond's witty black humour. But my friend couldn't find a film in it. I read the story once again, and felt an even stronger connection with the material than the previous time.

I knew Ruskin Saab since my *Blue Umbrella* days, so I called him to convey my desire to make a film on his short story, but only if he agreed to elaborate it into a novella. Each husband's character and the manner in which they were killed were very interesting and funny, but they needed to be fleshed out further. Ruskin Saab agreed to write the novella and I went away to shoot *Kaminey*, which I had been filming at that time.

While on the sets of *Kaminey* I started getting chapters from him, written in long hand and sealed in yellow envelopes with his address marked on the left bottom corner: Landour, Mussoorie. I felt so privileged to be the first and only reader of the legendary writer's new novella. Every time I got the yellow envelope, it turned me into a kid, and I eagerly waited for weeks to get the mail—smelling fresh, and containing a work of such suspense and humour—especially in this age of the Internet and emails. By the time I finished shooting *Kaminey*, I was sure *Susanna's Seven Husbands* would be my next film.

The second phase started when I sat with my co-writer from San Francisco, Matthew Robbins—my friend, philosopher and guide. Matthew started his career with Steven Spielberg's first feature film, *The Sugarland Express* (*Duel* was the film made for television, hence *The Sugarland Express* remains his first theatrical motion picture), and his latest is Guillermo Del Toro's *Don't Be Afraid of the Dark*. This is the right place for me to thank Matthew for whatever I have learned of screenwriting from him.

We went to Ooty to hunt for locations and crack the structure of the screenplay. And to our surprise we achieved it in nine days straight. Matthew then went back and wrote the first draft of the script, after which I wrote the second. Thereafter, it becomes difficult to pinpoint who wrote what. But the screenplay in this book is the draft we wrote together, from which I made the film *7 Khoon Maaf*.

The last phase came in filming the screenplay—bringing the characters to life from page to reality; discovering Susanna, her three servants (whom we referred to as the clean-up crew) and her seven precious husbands, or rather, seven precious specimens.

Film-making in general is a very strange process. Time after time you think that you have learned all there is to learn, and yet you are bound to find yourself struggling once more like a novice. Again I became a boy—ignorant, ambitious, less equipped, and yet confident of achieving the unachievable: inspiring the unit of 300-odd people, motivating them day and night to help me realize my dream. In every film I get this recurring thought during the shoot: 'Who asked you to be in this situation?'

One thing that can help push you through all this is the glimpse of the first screening, when you are watching your film with the audience for the very first time and the light goes dim. When silence descends from within for a few seconds before the first frame appears. In that moment you forget all the pain you have gone through. So many people contribute to the making of a film—from the lead actors to your assistants, the cameramen, the production designers, the costume designers, the sound engineers, right down to the production runners, the spot boys and so on—but the director walks away with all the credit. I wish I could thank each and every one by printing their names here.

As Gulzar Saab says, a film is made on two tables—initially on the writing table and later on the editing table. So you will find many elements in the script which are missing in the film. In fact, this book will offer readers a glimpse into a very unusual and unique process—of how a tale can be expanded from a short story into a novella and then transformed into a screenplay. Ruskin Saab gave me three alternate endings for the novella, but Matthew and I found a fourth one when we sat down to write the adaptation.

The sad part is that after working so intensely on a film for over a year, one loses objectivity towards one's own work. I try hard to remember the first impression I had of some of the incidents when I first read them in the book, but my memory fails me. The good part, however, is that each version of this incredible tale of Susanna and her seven husbands has its own individuality. So it will be difficult, I think, for the reader to choose or say which is better—the novella, the screenplay or the film.

VISHAL BHARDWAJ

SUSANNA'S SEVEN HUSBANDS

A novella by Ruskin Bond

EPISODE ONE

---

the major and the man-eater

I watched in fascination as a gigantic Black Widow spider, her body streaked with green and yellow, crept down the veranda wall in the direction of her sleeping husband. Her body was almost two inches in length, her slender black legs at least six inches long.

She was the boss-lady, the terror of the veranda walls. Like all spiders, she lived by murder, and her victims often included her own kind. Her husband, a paltry thing about half her size, lived almost entirely on her earnings. He was circumspect and kept out of her way, because he knew she would eat him when she was in the mood to do so.

I am watching as she moves like the minute-hand of a watch, each step a matter of thought, while all her eight eyes are focused on her victim. He is drowsy today, happily digesting the remains of a beetle slaughtered by his mistress earlier that day. She is bored with him, ready to terminate his aimless existence.

Suddenly she springs upon the hapless gentleman. There is a brief scuffle. Then she is tearing him to pieces and devouring him.

When her husband's life-blood has been sucked dry, his withered corpse falls to the ground. And the way is open for another.

That Black Widow spider always reminds me of Susanna, my lifelong friend and neighbour. Did I say 'friend'? Perhaps 'someone I knew well' would be a better description. The difference in our ages precluded us from being lovers, although I must say I found her beautiful even in her wicked old age. As I was never her husband, I have survived to tell this story.

I first saw her when I was twelve years old, living in the bungalow next door to her spacious estate on the outskirts of Meerut. In those days she had a little pony-drawn buggy in which she used to ride up and down the spacious Mall Road in the cantonment.

And when she went on shikar trips in the scrub forests along the Ganga Canal, she used a World War II jeep, driven by a dwarf of a man who also doubled as a jockey on one of her racehorses. In later years, she could be seen in a BMW or other swank automobile, always driven by her little jockey. But I mustn't jump the gun. Let me begin at the beginning, and the day I first saw this remarkable woman . . .

The guavas were ripe. They hung tantalizingly from the branches of the guava trees in the orchard behind the big house. No one seemed to be looking after them or gathering them for the market. What a waste! The temptation was too great for me. I scaled the wall that separated our bungalow from the big house, selected a tree that was easy to climb, and was soon in its branches devouring the luscious fruit. So intent was I on consuming as many guavas as my stomach could contain that I did not notice the approach of the rider on horseback until she was right before me, tapping her whip on her riding-boots and staring at me in obvious displeasure. She had raven-black hair, dark smouldering eyes, and the figure of an athlete. I guessed that she was about ten years older than me.

'Er—good morning, miss,' I stammered, a half-eaten guava falling from my hand.

'Good morning to you, sir. And what may you be doing in my guava trees?'

'Stealing guavas, miss.'

'An honest thief! The truth always has a certain authority about it. And you live next door, I think. No school today?'

'I skipped school, miss.'

She laughed—an infectious, devil-may-care laugh. 'I love your honesty, you little thief!' And she tapped her horse with her whip and cantered away in the direction of the house.

I hurried home, fearful that a report would be lodged with my parents. But next morning a little man wearing a jockey cap rode up in a buggy, ascended our veranda steps, and deposited a basket of guavas on the wicker table outside our front door. He said nothing—I discovered later that he was deaf and dumb—but gestured towards the big house and gave me to understand that they were a gift from his mistress, the mysterious woman who owned the orchard. Before I could say anything, he gave me a quick salute, and with a wicked grin returned to his buggy and rode away.

'Who sent you all these guavas?' asked my mother.

'The lady next door,' I said. 'I met her yesterday.'

'She must be a very kind person,' said my mother.

Yes, she was kind to children and animals, as I was to discover. And kind even to odd creatures and freaks like the dwarf who had brought me the guavas. Her cruelty was reserved for another species of human.

Susanna Anna-Maria Johannes was her full name. She was of Dutch and East Indian descent. Her grandfather had made his fortune in indigo, and her father had trained and bred racehorses with some success. Her mother had died when she was an infant, and she had been brought up by her father, who had taught her to ride, look after the horses, and run the estate. Upon his death, a year before I met her, she inherited the property, the horses and considerable wealth in the form of 'treasure' which, the gossips said, was hidden away in some underground chamber on the estate.

She had servants, and a pair of greyhounds who often followed her when she rode about the grounds, but no one in the neighbourhood had been inside the rambling old mansion.

Her father had been an unsociable, grumpy old man whose life had revolved around the racecourse. He had discouraged visitors, and Susanna had grown up in the company of dogs, horses and domestic servants.

Sometimes she would pass me on the road, and she would acknowledge my greeting with a fleeting smile or a wave of the hand. Every week she would visit the Wheeler Club to borrow a book from its lending library, and it was there that she met Major Mehta, an officer in one of the regiments posted in Meerut. He was a good ten years older than Susanna, but he had a charming manner, and his good looks were enhanced by a Jackie-Shroff-type moustache and the long legs of an Amitabh Bachchan. 'You ought to be in the movies,' said his fellow officers in jest. 'Maybe I will, one day,' he'd reply, for he was rather vain.

Susanna, unaccustomed to male company, was soon bowled over by the handsome Major, who took her to parties and dances and shopping sprees to Delhi, where it was Susanna who did most of the spending.

He was soon sharing her buggy, and one day when they stopped outside her front gate, I happened to come along on my bicycle. I got down and greeted Susanna in my polite schoolboy fashion. She turned to the Major and said, 'You must meet my young friend and neighbour. He's good at climbing trees.'

'Hello, young man,' said the Major rather patronizingly. 'And what's your name?'

'Arun,' I said. 'And what's yours?'

'Hari Mehta. And Susanna here will soon be Mrs Mehta.'

This was news to me and it was also news to the little jockey-driver who had just come up to take charge of the buggy as its occupants got down. The 'Goonga', as he was known, looked from his mistress to the Major, and when his eyes settled on the Major they were filled with a hatred the intensity of which I had not seen before.

'Congratulations, sir,' I said.

'And you will come to the wedding, I hope,' said Susanna.

'Of course, miss.'

∾

But I did not attend the wedding. They were married in the magistrate's office, and this was followed by a reception in the regimental mess. The liquor flowed freely, and the couple's health and happiness was the subject of a number of toasts. The couple spent their honeymoon in Mussoorie, occupying the best suite in the Savoy. Susanna paid for it, of course. And on their return to Meerut, the Major lost no time in urging upon Susanna the necessity of having a joint account. 'Either, or Survivor'!

The Major had every intention of being a survivor, and even managed to avoid a posting in a sensitive border area, where there was an occasional exchange of fire. Not that the Major disliked guns. He was something of a shikari, by his own account, and boasted of having disposed of more than one man-eating tiger, two leopards and a crocodile. Actually, Susanna knew more about wild animals and shikar than the Major, having often accompanied her father into the jungles around Dehra and Bijnor. Sometimes they had been accompanied by a friend of her father's, a certain Jim Corbett, and Susanna had picked up a fair amount of jungle-craft from him.

The Major did not invite any of his fellow officers over to their home. Soon after the marriage, a streak of jealousy had become apparent in his nature.

He resented the admiring looks that Susanna received from men younger than him, and if one of his colleagues invited them over for a dinner or a get-together, he would refuse, even before Susanna could get a word in. He was even jealous of the servants, especially those like the Goonga, who were in the confidence of their mistress. He would constantly find fault with the jockey, and urge Susanna to get rid of him.

But he was a good jockey, often winning races in Meerut or Delhi, and Susanna needed his help in running the stables. Moreover, he was devoted to her, and while Susanna did not find him physically attractive, she valued his loyalty.

The little jockey hated the Major. All the servants resented him. Susanna, too, was soon regretting her alliance with this boring and egotistic man. There is no more tiresome a creature than a jealous husband, suspicious of everyone who tries to be friendly. He was even jealous of me—wouldn't stop, if Susanna wanted to talk to me; ignored me, even if I greeted them on the road.

One day, as I was cycling back from school, I passed their gate just as the Major and Susanna emerged—not in their buggy, but in her old Army jeep. In the back seat were the jockey and the gardener, Shah Rukh. Both carried guns—a rifle, and a .12-bore shotgun. Susanna was driving.

She stopped when she saw me, smiled and said, 'We're off on a shikar trip. Like to come?'

'Some day,' I said. 'I'd have to ask my parents.'

'Children shouldn't be on a shikar trip,' said the Major. 'Too dangerous. Especially when there's a man-eater around.'

The party drove off, and I did not see them for two or three days. In fact, I did not see the Major again. His remains were not suitable for 'children' to view.

I heard the sad story from Shah Rukh, who had been quite friendly ever since I'd been given the freedom of the guava orchard. He spoke to me over the garden wall.

'Here you heard about what happened to the Major-sahib?' he asked.

'No. Did he shoot the tiger?'

'The tiger got the Major. Miss Susanna is very upset.'

'What happened?'

And this is what happened, according to Shah Rukh, who was present when the tragedy took place.

They had set up a machaan on a big shisham tree, and had made themselves comfortable with their guns and some provisions. The Major had brought along his favourite brand of whisky. A goat had been tied to the foot of the tree as bait. If the man-eater came along, it would not have been particularly interested in a mutton dinner; but if it was really hungry it might be tempted to kill and eat the goat in lieu of something better.

Shah Rukh was something of a shikari himself and had often accompanied Susanna on her hunting trips. He had joined them on the machaan, but it was the Major who had been given the privilege of shooting the tiger. Shah Rukh sensed the inexperience of the Major and was ready to use the second gun if necessary. This gun was kept between him and Susanna; so both of them had their hands free.

As the evening wore on, the Major felt increasingly thirsty. He was in the habit of drinking two or three whiskies every evening, and it was now well past cocktail time. The sun had set; a quarter-moon was in the sky. The Major took out his small whisky glass and poured himself a stiff drink.

The tiger was in the vicinity, and it was aware of the tethered goat. It also knew that there were humans around; it could smell them on the night wind. The tiger was prepared to wait. If the humans were on foot, it would rather have one of them instead of a skinny old goat.

The Major poured himself a second drink.

'Won't you have one too, darling?' he whispered to Susanna.

She shook her head. 'We must be very still. Very quiet. Or the tiger will not come.'

At midnight the Major poured himself a third drink. And at midnight the tiger approached the clearing. Its eyes glowed in the dark. Susanna could see them, but she said nothing.

'Be ready, sahib,' whispered Shah Rukh. 'The tiger is approaching.'

Suddenly the bushes parted and the tiger made its charge.

But it did not go for the goat. A mighty leap, and it was almost in the machaan. It missed the platform by inches and fell backwards. Major Mehta lurched forward, the whisky glass dropping from his hand. He reached for his gun, but he was already off-balance. The tree was still shaking from the impact of the animal's charge. The Major toppled over, fell out of the tree, and landed near the bleating goat.

Immediately the tiger was upon him.

Snarls, shouts, screams rent the air as the big cat dragged its screaming victim into the bushes. There were more screams, gradually dying away. Then there was silence, broken only by the bleating of the terrified goat.

Shah Rukh and the Goonga and several forest guards spent two days looking for the Major, while Susanna waited patiently but not too sorrowfully in the Forest Rest House.

Eventually, they found what was left of the Major: a few bones, his boots, his shredded clothes—not enough for a good funeral pyre.

Had he fallen of his own volition, or had he been given a little assistance from behind? Had he drunk too much, or had something been added to his whisky? These questions did not arise at the time, but they were to bother me later on.

EPISODE TWO

enter the beetle

'Won't you come into my parlour,' said the spider to the fly, and many a fly has found its way into the jaws of the Black Widow spider on my veranda wall.

But today there's a bonus, an extra savoury on the menu.

A pretty green beetle, sparkling like an emerald, has blundered straight into that intricate web in the corner of my veranda. Our friendly neighbourhood spider loves beetles. A beetle to a spider is like strawberries and cream to a human. Except that spiders can dispense with the cream.

Our Black Widow loses no time in collecting her breakfast. She tears that little beetle apart and sucks it dry of its strawberry juices. Only the outer covering remains, hanging forlornly from that finely-spun web.

Mohan Prakash, stage name Jimmy Rogers, wanted to be a Beetle. That is, the singing kind. For he was a great fan of the group that called itself the Beatles, and he felt that he could sing as well as any of them; which was probably true, since real musical ability was not among their accomplishments.

Jimmy also possessed a guitar, and wherever Jimmy went, the guitar was sure to go.

He had performed once at our school, but the students had started singing instead, and had drowned him out. He had also sung and played his guitar in a church, but had not been invited to come again. He was sitting on the lawn of the Wheeler Club, playing sad songs for himself, when Susanna heard him and, feeling sorry for him, clapped and complimented him on his singing. Almost immediately, he was on his feet, begging to sing another song for her.

This was about a year after the loss of her husband, the Major, to the man-eating tiger. I hadn't seen much of her in that time, as my holidays were spent playing cricket. She now used a car instead of the buggy, as she had become rather conscious of the inquisitive glances of passers-by.

But I had become quite friendly with Shah Rukh, the gardener, and one afternoon, while Susanna was out shopping, he took me on a round of the grounds, which were very extensive.

Well behind the house were the stables, where the horses were kept. There were three racehorses here, all in prime condition. They were looked after by a couple of syces, but only the dumb jockey was permitted to take them out for rides. Susanna had her favourite horse, a beautiful black stallion, and she had ridden him herself in a couple of races, much to the resentment and outrage of the male members of the racing fraternity.

'Now let me show you something interesting, Arun bhai,' said Shah Rukh, taking me by the hand and leading me through some thick shrubbery to a part of the estate that was not visible from the main road. We came upon a large tank, the water covered with floating lotus leaves and flowers. On all sides there were steps leading down to the water, but I did not dare go down any of them, because on almost every step there were several snakes, basking in the sun or gliding in and out of the water.

'Why do you keep so many snakes?' I asked. 'Why don't you get rid of them?'

'Miss Susanna is fond of them. And they are used to her. She can go down those steps without being harmed.'

'Are they not poisonous, then?'

'They are all poisonous to some extent. They are vipers, and they have increased in numbers over the years. But they do not go far from this spot. They like it here. Plenty of frogs to feed on! But come, I will show you one that is really poisonous.'

And taking me by the hand he led me to the far corner of the boundary wall, where a small temple was set into a narrow gap between the wall and the trunk of a pipal tree.

'It's a Naag Temple,' said Shah Rukh. 'Every morning, the miss-sahib or her maid-servant leaves a saucer of milk outside, and the cobra, who lives here, comes out for a drink. See, the saucer is empty. That means he has come and gone.'

But apparently the resident cobra did not go too far from his abode. Even as we turned away, the tall grass began to sway, and a huge cobra rose from the undergrowth, its hooded head swaying from side to side.

'Do not be afraid,' he said. 'It is just looking to see if you have brought it something.'

'Another day,' I said, as I backed away. 'But I thought Susanna was a Christian.'

'So she is, when she visits the church. But her mother was a devout Hindu lady, who made this little Naag Temple. And the miss-sahib keeps up the tradition of feeding the cobra.'

'And her father—what was he?'

'Oh, he did not believe in anything. He did not care much for religion. Never went to a place of worship. But he was tolerant of all religions. We are of many faiths here. I believe in the one true God, as you know.'

'And the Goonga?'

'Oh, he is of a strange forest tribe. He believes in magic and spirits and animal sacrifices. Don't make an enemy of him—he will put a curse on you.'

He led me away from the temple and around to the front of the house.

'It is getting late,' he said, 'and Miss Susanna will soon be here. I cannot take you inside the house—that is forbidden. But she likes you, and one day she may invite you in. There are secret places in parts of the house. Even I have not seen them. But look who's here—a new hero to entertain us.'

Sitting on the low wall around the garden well was Jimmy the Beetle, strumming his guitar. 'Won't you sing for us?' asked Shah Rukh.

'I don't sing for servants,' said the troubadour. 'And I play the guitar for myself.' He stopped playing.

'My friend here is not a servant,' said Shah Rukh.

'He plays very badly,' I said. 'See, even the crows have flown away.'

Shah Rukh accompanied me to the front gate, and as I turned into the road, Susanna arrived in her small car. She slowed down at the gate and greeted me in the friendliest manner. She was looking prettier than ever.

'You're growing fast,' she said. 'One of these days I'll take you to the races. You'll get rich betting on my horse.'

She drove up to the front of the house, and the Beetle rose from his perch and greeted her with a bow.

I went home and took a nap. An hour or two later, when I looked over the wall, the Beetle was still there, sitting on the veranda steps and singing to Susanna, who was reclining on one of the veranda's rocking chairs. I could hear the words of his song quite distinctly.

'*Oh Susanna, please don't cry for me,*
I'll wait for you in heaven,
with my banjo on my knee.'

It was an adaptation of an old Western folk song. Jimmy did not sing it very well, but the sentiment must have pleased Susanna, because she clapped enthusiastically at the end. As for Jimmy, he did not know how prophetic his words would prove to be.

A few weeks later they were married in the little church that the Begum Samru had built a hundred and fifty years earlier. Not far from it were the graves of two of the several husbands that the amorous begum had sent to their Maker. Not that Susanna intended following in the begum's footsteps. She seemed genuinely fond of her romantic rock singer, and did her best to promote his singing career.

She arranged for him to perform at the Imperial in Delhi, and the Savoy in Mussoorie. He sang his heart out, gyrated like Presley, and in his frenzy smashed two guitars. (Since he now had a collection of guitars, all provided by Susanna, this hardly mattered.) The response was lukewarm.

'Perhaps you were not meant to be a Beetle,' said Susanna sympathetically. 'All that long hair doesn't suit you. And the hippies will soon be out of fashion. Why don't you become a cowboy singer? You'll look great in a cowboy outfit.'

So Jimmy had a haircut, took to wearing boots, jeans, a leather jacket, and a wide-brimmed cowboy hat. His repertoire underwent a change too. Now he sang Folk instead of Rock—sang the Blues, sang ballads of the old West: 'Oh Bury Me on the Lone Prairie', 'Don't Fence Me In', and 'Keep Cool, Fool'—but that didn't work either. People were staying away from his performances, or walking out in the middle of them, and the hotel managements were not pleased.

'He sings all right,' said one manager. 'But he doesn't have sex appeal. Maybe he should go to Bombay and get a little experience there.'

So Susanna sent him to Bombay, hoping he might get into films. He was sent to various producers, and they were all happy to give him a screen test. After all, he had a rich wife and she might just agree to bank-roll a film if her husband was in it!

But not only did Jimmy lack sex appeal, he also lacked any sort of acting ability. Nobody wanted him.

Keeping Jimmy in a flat in Bombay was proving costly, and after six unproductive months Susanna came to Bombay to collect her singing spouse. She was immediately offered roles in several films! Her good looks and striking personality bowled everyone over. Poor Jimmy was weighed down by an inferiority complex.

Susanna was not interested in a career in films or in being the toast of Bombay society. Her home and her horses called her. She bundled Jimmy into a plane and flew with him back to Delhi. Her car was waiting for them at the airport and two hours later they were in Meerut.

∽

Jimmy sulked. Another month in Bombay, he said, and he would have broken into films. He had been about to abandon his Western outfit and adopt a more traditional Indian costume for his act.

'It would have made no difference,' said Susanna. 'Perhaps you should do something else. Would you like a job at the racecourse? They need a new secretary.'

'I hate horses,' said Jimmy.

'I can get you a car agency.'

'I hate cars.'

Susanna had to admit to herself that Jimmy did lack sex appeal. He was half-hearted, almost apologetic in his love-making, and sometimes she felt that he would rather be in bed with a guitar.

'What on earth did I see in him in the first place?' she asked herself. 'And what do I do with him now?'

Jimmy did not know what to do with himself. He mooned about the grounds and strummed listlessly on his guitar, but his heart was not in his music. He could not even sing, now that not even Susanna wanted to listen to him. Depressed, he went to a local chemist and asked for something to lift him out of his depression. He went home, swallowed a Dexedrine, and cheered up a little.

He was on this chemical for two or three weeks, but whenever the effect wore off he was more depressed than before.

Early one summer morning I was up at the break of dawn, woken by the shouts of two of my school friends who had come to fetch me for a cricket match in a neighbouring town. I dressed, and shouted to my mother to give me some breakfast. Then, out of pure habit, I looked over the wall—and there, hanging from a branch and swaying slightly in the dawn breeze, was a man—or rather his corpse. I recognized Jimmy from his clothes, and from the fact that his guitar lay on the grass, a few feet away from his dangling body.

EPISODE THREE

portrait of susanna

Jimmy Prakash had the honour of being buried beside Begum Samru's lovers. 'Beloved husband of Susanna' went the inscription on the tombstone. And his favourite guitar was buried with him. That was a nice touch, suggested by Susanna.

But the matter did not end there. A hanging, even if it's suicide, has to be investigated by the police, and even before Jimmy had been cut down, Deputy Superintendent Keemat Lal was at the scene, examining the body and looking for clues. Jimmy had hanged himself with a cord, apparently a nylon curtain cord, and there was a deep indentation on his neck where the cord had dug into his flesh. But there were other marks, according to the doctor who conducted the autopsy. There were bruises on the throat, probably caused by the pressure of a hand or hands. Had he been strangled first, and then hoisted into the tree to make it appear as though he had hanged himself? It would have taken strong hands to choke the life out of the young man.

DSP Keemat Lal investigated the ground around the tree. I watched from the sidelines. I had been the first on the scene, had given the alarm. It had rained that night, and the footprints of my running shoes could be seen quite clearly. But there were other footprints too. The prints of Susanna's riding boots, of Shah Rukh's chappals—and also the print of a large bare foot.

Keemat Lal spent a lot of time studying this particular imprint.

'Come over here, young man,' he called to me. 'You seem to be an intelligent boy. Do you notice anything unusual about this footprint?'

I stared at it for some time. 'It's a broad foot,' I said. 'Not long but splayed, like a labourer's.'

'Well done, Dr Watson,' he said. Obviously he was a student of the methods of Sherlock Holmes. 'But is there anything else? Something unusual?'

I stared at the footprint a little longer, then exclaimed, 'There are six toes! This foot has an extra toe.'

'Well done! You'll make a good detective!'

And DSP Keemat Lal set about examining the feet of everyone on the premises—including mine.

None of them matched the six-toed footprint. Shah Rukh had normal feet. Goonga, the jockey, was pigeon-toed, but there were only five of them. The syces also passed muster.

'Perhaps it was a thief who came over the wall,' I said.

'Possibly,' said Keemat Lal, but he wasn't satisfied.

During the next few days he made several visits to the house, questioning the servants and drinking innumerable cups of tea with Susanna on her front veranda. She showed him around the grounds and parts of the house. He admired her horses, her garden, her family heirlooms; but he felt that she had not shown him everything. Where did her wealth come from, he wondered. Was it only from racehorses? Or did she have assets that no one knew about? There were limits to his prying. She was not under suspicion of a crime. She did not mind talking to him, and he enjoyed being in her company.

And I, too, found myself spending more time with Susanna. I was now going on fifteen, an age at which an adolescent is susceptible to the attentions of a beautiful woman.

I can still see her clearly in my mind's eye—slender and dark-haired, with a smile so warm that it could have melted a Himalayan glacier. She did not use make-up, but I can recall her delicate perfume—a flowery garden fragrance. And

I'll never forget the gold bracelet she always wore, whether she was in slacks or skirt or sari. Her father had given her a string of pearls—real pearls—on her sixteenth birthday, and she wore them on most occasions: at the Club, or at the races, or on social occasions which she could not avoid. Nor can I forget her laughter. Sometimes it had a mocking quality; at other times it expressed her sensuality and joy in being alive.

༄

I was to attend a boarding school in the hills for the final year of my schooling, but before I left I paid a visit to the nearby town of Sardhana in the company of two of my cricket-playing friends.

It rained all day and the match was cancelled, so we passed the time by looking around the palace and the cathedral built by the Begum Samru, the lady who had ruled over the rich agricultural province for half a century.

The widow of Sombre, a German soldier of fortune, she had inherited the Jagir of Sardhana gifted to her husband by the Mughal Emperor for 'services rendered'. Some said the begum was of noble lineage; others, that she was a Kashmiri dancing-girl. Beautiful in her youth, she had lived to the age of ninety, going through a succession of lovers and husbands before becoming a devout Catholic and leaving her fortune to various religious and charitable institutions. Childless all her life, she had adopted her young nephew who had helped her to look after the estate and keep some of her fortune-hunting lovers in check.

My friends and I visited the fine old church and admired the statue of the begum, seated on her 'throne'. She looked a bit like Queen Victoria, but not as plump. In the nearby cemetery we came across the neglected and broken tombs of the many European mercenaries who had served under the begum, training her small standing army and occasionally leading it into battle against neighbouring rajas and warlords.

RUSKIN BOND

These officers of the begum—French, German, Irish—were an ill-educated lot whose only aim was to get rich. Some found favour with the begum. She went through several husbands, all of whom came to sticky ends, if not on the field of battle then in their beds. The begum tired quickly of her many lovers, who proved to be unsatisfactory in more ways than one. Had she been blessed with a child of her own, things might have been different . . .

All this I had learned from my history teacher, and I was eager to tell him that I had seen the begum's statue and portrait.

The portrait hung in the office of the old palace, now a school. The nun in charge allowed us to see it. It was a large portrait, the head life-size, and it must have been painted when the begum was about forty. She had just the suggestion of a smile, and a cruel one at that; but her eyes were large and lustrous, and she had a strong, rather determined chin, finely arched eyebrows, and full, sensuous lips.

I had a feeling that I had seen her before. Where? When?

'What do you think of her?' I asked my friend.

'I prefer Rekha,' said Siddharth.

'She reminds me of one of my aunts,' said Rahul.

'She reminds me of someone too,' I said.

And then it struck me. The begum bore a close resemblance to Susanna. Or to be precise—Susanna resembled the begum. The same forehead, the same eyes, the same full lips and lustrous hair.

It made me wonder. Could Susanna have been a descendant of Begum Samru—descended from her adopted nephew or some other relative?

Or perhaps the resemblance was just coincidence.

And then another thought struck me. Was there, after all, something in the belief in reincarnation? And did the soul of the begum reside in Susanna?

EPISODE FOUR

farewell to a prince

I was away for over a year, completing my schooling in Simla. I came home with some fluff on my cheeks and the beginnings of a moustache. I was tall for my age, and I had developed into a fast bowler.

I had expected to see Susanna, but several days passed without any sign of her. Then I encountered Shah Rukh on the footpath outside their gate.

'Where is Miss Susanna?' I asked.

'Mrs Susanna, you mean. No, it's Princess Susanna. Or Susanna Rani. I call her Rani Ma!'

'What do you mean?'

'Why, hadn't you heard? Our lady has married the Prince of Purkazi. They have gone up to Mussoorie for their honeymoon.'

'Well, that was quick. It's just over a year since the Beetle passed away.'

'Well, he's a fast worker, our Prince. And our lady was getting restless.'

'Is the Prince handsome?' (I have to admit I felt a twinge of jealousy.) 'He must be very rich.'

'I don't know about being rich, but he is handsome. A bit like Dev Anand.'

'Oh. And otherwise what is he like?'

'*Akru*-type. Nose in the air. Thinks too much of himself. Don't know why she married him.'

'Maybe she likes Dev Anand.'

'Then she should have married a film star. And we could all have gone to Bombay.'

'The Goonga will be in demand there,' I said. 'They are short of dwarfs. By the way, where is he?'

'He has gone up with them. He has to look after the cars. There are two cars now. And Maggie has gone too.'

Maggie was Susanna's maidservant—middle-aged, grumpy, ugly, and a great gossip. But very efficient.

Shah Rukh told me that Susanna had met the Prince on one of her trips to the Delhi Races. He had won some money on one of her horses and had gone over to the stalls to congratulate the jockey. As the jockey was the Goonga, the only response was a grin that was more like a grimace. The Prince turned away, only to find himself face-to-face with Susanna.

The attraction was mutual. He invited her out to dinner. Then to a musical soirée. They went to a recital of ghazals sung by one of the country's top ghazal singers, and Susanna decided that she preferred ghazals to the Beatles. Towards the end of the recital the Prince proposed marriage to Susanna. Under the heady influence of the music, she accepted.

They were married a month later, but did not spend much time at Susanna's ancestral home. The Prince had an old house, or 'palace' as he called it, in Mussoorie, and it was there that they spent their honeymoon.

It turned out to be a long honeymoon, and a disastrous one at that.

೪

The monsoon had broken, and it had been raining heavily for several days. Having finished with school, I was now the proud owner of a scooter, but it did not prevent me from getting drenched, as I rode home from the bazaar. I was almost home when I saw Susanna's car turn in at the main gate. The Goonga was at the wheel, and Maggie sat beside him. In the back seat sat Susanna, looking very pale and tired. Of the Prince there was no sign, nor did another car arrive.

Susanna saw me, but she did not wave to me, as was her custom. Instead, she looked straight ahead, her face expressionless.

Next day, when the weather cleared, I called out to Shah Rukh and asked him what had happened. Where was the Prince? Why had Susanna returned alone?

Shah Rukh was only too anxious to bring me up to date.

'The Prince is dead,' he announced quite casually.

He lost no time in telling me all that he knew, and it was quite a lot, since he had got all the details from Maggie. And according to her, it was good riddance of a bad prince.

The honeymoon had started off well enough, with drives down to the Jumna, or to Rishikesh and Hardwar. There was a picnic at Kempty Falls and a moonlight party at Hathi Paon. But as a lover the Prince left much to be desired. If he tried to be loving and romantic, he was ineffective, impotent. He could only get excited if he became rough and violent. Susanna found this tiresome, not to say humiliating. After two or three nights of being knocked around, she refused to sleep with the Prince and shut herself up in her own room.

He tried various remedies for his inadequacy—ayurvedic, yunani, allopathic—but nothing seemed to work. His condition, after all, was psychological. Maggie had guessed the truth and did her best to help matters by sending for a country hakim who guaranteed success with his pure and costly *saand-ka-tel*—the oil of a certain rock lizard that was found in the hills.

'Not only will your pleasure increase,' he promised, 'but you will find yourself equipped with a veritable *hamaam-dasta*.'

The combination of *saand-ka-tel* and the Prince's own sadistic nature resulted in a nightmarish experience for Susanna. Having—in his most charming manner—persuaded her to sleep in his room, he started off by being tender and passionate, but his brain would not send the right message to his loins, and he found himself as ineffective as before.

'It's all your fault!' he swore at Susanna. 'You're as cold as a marble statue.'

And he proceeded to beat her, first with his open hands and then with his fists. Only then was he able to perform.

Next morning Susanna appeared alone at the breakfast table, the bruises on her face and arms visible to all. Maggie saw them, the Goonga saw them, and so did the Prince's attendants. Susanna confided in Maggie. Maggie used sign language to convey a message to the Goonga. He slunk off, his face dark as thunder.

The Prince did not emerge till noon. He could not face Susanna. He told one of his servants that he was going for a drive, and he took his own car and drove off by himself.

∽

The road to Dhanolti winds round several steep mountains, with cliffs and precipices along the way. The road twists and turns, and there are sudden dips and rises which test the skills of the best drivers. There are no parapets, only a whitewashed drum here and there to mark the edge of the road.

The Prince was in a terrible temper. He was angry with his wife, with himself, with the world. Here he was—a handsome young Prince, the envy of all. But he didn't have the one thing that would make him happy—a normal sex drive. He cursed the cars on the road, he cursed the mules and the drivers, he cursed the day he was born.

There was a sudden descent near Dhanolti. The car gathered speed. A mule stood in the middle of the road. The Prince pressed hard on the brake, but there was no let-up in the speed of the car.

'Damn!' he cursed. 'Someone's been fiddling with the brakes.'

Someone had indeed tampered with the brakes.

The car swerved to avoid the mule. But its momentum took it off the road and over the edge. There were no trees here to break its fall. It sailed into space like a beautiful toy spacecraft, and then it fell. And, like a toy, it was smashed to pieces on the rocks over a hundred feet below.

Hours later, when the villagers reached the wreck, they found the driver slumped on the broken bonnet, himself a broken doll.

EPISODE FIVE

enter the diplomat

That spider on my wall was getting restless. It was some time since she'd dined off a fat, juicy male. Now she was thinking of moving her web elsewhere . . .

~

Not immediately, though.

A few years were to pass before Susanna took up the challenge of another husband. She did not seem to age. Although thirty, she could have passed for twenty-five. Being childless might have had something to do with it. As for me, I was now twenty-one, pursuing a BA in History from Delhi University.

As I was in and out of Meerut quite a lot, I saw Susanna quite often during those years. She had even invited me into the house on two or three occasions, had shown me the family heirlooms—period furniture, old Chinese vases, Mughal miniatures, family portraits, shikar trophies from the time of the Raj—but she did not show me her jewellery, and there were one or two locked rooms which were always locked, according to Shah Rukh.

It was difficult to be alone with Susanna. Maggie was always hovering nearby. After the experience of the prince, she suspected all men of being monsters, and her suspicious glances gave me to understand that she wasn't going to be fooled by my innocent good looks. Even though I was many years younger than Susanna, Maggie suspected my intentions!

Not that she was above suspicion.

She usually wore slippers, but on one occasion, when it was raining heavily, she ran out of the house to bring in some clothes that had been left outside to dry. I was standing in the veranda, waiting to see Susanna, when Maggie came running back with the clothes. She happened to be barefoot, and as she stood at the top of the steps, recovering from her exertions, I looked at her wide, splayed feet—and saw that there were six toes on her left foot!

Immediately my mind went back to that morning when I had discovered Jimmy's body hanging in the guava orchard. DSP Keemat Lal had arrived on the scene, and had observed that a footprint nearby clearly showed six toes. He had examined everyone's feet, but where had Maggie been that day? Obviously she had made herself scarce.

Of course it was possible that she had been in the orchard the previous evening. Then why disappear during the investigation? She knew something, even if she was not the culprit.

But it was a long time ago, and there seemed no point in pursuing the matter now. Even DSP Keemat Lal had moved on to another district. And there was much else to occupy our minds.

The diplomat was Signor Eduardo Romero, chargé d'affaires at a South American embassy. He was thirty-five, tall and handsome, though inclined to be diabetic. It was said that he had been a bullfighter once, then a cattle rancher, before entering his country's diplomatic service. In his leisure time he liked to carry a whip and to demonstrate his skill with it. He was a part-time artist, and it was at an exhibition of his paintings in Delhi that he met Susanna.

Whenever Susanna was in Delhi she visited one or two of

RUSKIN BOND

the art galleries. She did not buy paintings—her home was cluttered with old paintings, most of them English hunting scenes collected by her father—but she liked to look at what was new in the art world, and she particularly liked Signor Romero's studies of horses. One painting in particular pleased her—a charming study of a mare with her foal.

She had been standing before the picture for some time when someone behind her said, 'You like this picture, mademoiselle?'

Standing before her was the artist himself, Signor Romero, sporting a short French beard and a rakish-looking hat.

'Yes, it's beautiful,' said Susanna. 'I love horses, and you have captured the grace of the adult and the awkwardness of the colt . . . Are you the artist?'

'At your service! Would you like to have the picture?'

'Normally I don't buy pictures, but I love this one.'

'Then it is yours. A gift from the artist to a beautiful woman who can appreciate beauty in a beast. But on one condition.'

'Yes.'

'That you have lunch with me. There's an Italian restaurant just opened in one of the new hotels. Please be my guest. And the picture will be delivered to you next week, as soon as my exhibition is over.'

∽

A week later the picture was delivered by Signor Romero himself, who drove down to Meerut in his imported sports car, bringing with him not only the painting (which was hung in Susanna's study, above her desk) but also a hamper packed with chocolates, cheese, salami and other delicacies, and several bottles of the choicest wines.

A picnic was held in the orchard. It was November, just the right month for a picnic.

'Would you like to join us?' Susanna called out to me from across the wall.

'Another time,' I said. 'I have to finish writing a dissertation.' It looked like a very private picnic, and I did not think the Signor would have welcomed my presence.

Over the next two or three months those picnics became a regular feature, the Signor driving down from Delhi every weekend. He attended one of the races, admired Susanna's horses—'Now I know why you liked my paintings!'—and took an instant dislike to Susanna's little jockey, the Goonga. He seemed to dislike dwarfs in general and dumb ones in particular.

Signor Romero had a wife and children tucked away in Peru or Bolivia—something that Susanna only discovered much later. A little bigamy did not bother the good Signor. He took Susanna on a holiday to Goa, and he proposed to her while they were swimming together in a little cove along the coast. They made love in the pool. As a lover the Signor had no shortcomings, and Susanna was happy to accompany him to the altar.

They returned to Meerut very briefly, and then were off on an extended honeymoon to Mauritius, Capri, the Canary Islands and the Bahamas. Obviously the Signor had a 'thing' about islands.

He also had diabetes, although you wouldn't have thought so from looking at him. He looked the picture of rude health, a horseman and an athlete, but he had blacked out more than once, and he complained at times of pain and tiredness in his legs.

It had become necessary for him to be given an insulin injection every day, and this was administered by Susanna, who became quite expert at filling the syringe and then inserting the needle without causing any discomfort or pain.

When they returned to Delhi, there was the usual round of parties, attended by diplomats, politicians, retired bureaucrats, and the upper echelons of Delhi society.

Naturally I did not see much of Susanna during this period, as her trips to Meerut were infrequent and brief. The estate seemed to run quite well on its own, with the Goonga looking after the stables, Maggie looking after the house, and Shah Rukh taking care of the grounds.

However, after a hectic party season, both Susanna and Signor Romero felt the need of a rest, and returned to Meerut for a month of peace and quiet.

It was quiet enough, but peace did not reign for long.

Signor Romero was rude to the servants, and treated them as serfs. He was used to dealing with the humble, poverty-stricken peons of Mexico, Bolivia and Peru. They could be bullied, even thrashed, if they did not please their masters. Susanna's servants, if you could call them that, were not in the habit of being pushed around. Going for an early morning ride, the Signor had fallen from his horse because the saddle had not been strapped on properly. He had proceeded to thrash the young syce, using the handle of his whip. The boy had not retaliated, but the Goonga arrived just then, and raising his riding-whip, had threatened the Signor.

'Oh, it's a whipping contest you want, is it?' sneered Signor Romero, who hated the little jockey, as indeed he hated anyone with a physical defect. 'Come on, then! Let's see who is better with a whip. I'll lend you one of mine!'

Although the Goonga was hard of hearing, he understood what the Signor meant, and he did not decline the challenge. He had a long whip of his own, a leather-thonged 'hunter'—the sort that is sold by hawkers outside the Agra Fort.

A small crowd assembled to see the duel, and I had a clear view of the encounter from the boundary wall.

Some ten or twelve spectators had formed a large circle, and in that circle the two men, stripped to the waist, were fighting a duel! A duel of a kind that I had never before witnessed or even dreamed of. They were fighting with their whips—the Signor with his South American stock-whip, the little jockey with his 'hunter'.

The cruel leather thongs, some ten feet long, were hissing and curling through the air like venomous snakes. As I gazed, astounded, a lash snapped around the neck of the Goonga with a horrible crack. Instantly a gush of blood spurted from the small man's flesh and I saw that the skin had been cut away as with a razor. It was horrible!

The ferocity of both fighters, fuelled by their hatred of each other, was almost inhuman. Wherever the lash curled and struck, a fiery cut marked the impact. Both appeared insensible to pain, but I realized that the little jockey was no match for his tormentor . . . I soon realized that the Signor's object was to cut out his opponent's eyes, and as I watched, I saw a thin snaky thong curl and flicker round the little man's face. He could not curse as his opponent was cursing, he could barely cry out. But he staggered to and fro, grunting and moaning in agony, with his hands pressed to his face.

The Signor straightened up, coiled his whiplash round his arm, and calmly walked away. The little crowd melted away.

I slipped to the ground and ran towards the scene of the fight, where I found the Goonga lying on the ground, unconscious, his body slashed to ribbons and drenched in blood.

Shah Rukh was approaching from the opposite direction. I yelled to him to fetch Susanna, and then I made a dash for the road and stopped a passing taxi. Shah Rukh ran back to say that Susanna was at the club, and that he'd phoned and left a message for her. Together we lifted the Goonga into the taxi, and twenty minutes later we had him in the emergency ward of the local hospital.

'At least one of his eyes has gone,' said the doctor.

'As he's deaf and dumb that doesn't leave him with much,' I said.

'And he'll be scarred for life,' added the doctor.

'He was not much to look at, anyway,' said Shah Rukh. 'But will he live?'

'He's tough, he'll pull through.'

When Susanna arrived, she found the Goonga swathed and wrapped in bandages; only his mouth and nose were visible. The doctor informed us that he was delirious and that morphine had been administered.

'Do all you can for him, doctor,' said Susanna. 'Spare no expense.'

And abruptly she turned on her heels and walked out of the ward. But I had seen the expression on her face. I would not have cared to be her enemy at that moment.

∼

What happened next we heard from Maggie.

There was a quarrel, of course. Susanna's voice was raised in fury. The little jockey had been her father's favourite, and she was outraged at the treatment that had been meted out to him. The Signor shrugged, and tried to laugh off the incident. Such duels were common enough in his own country, he said; nothing to get excited about. He ate his dinner with relish, and went to bed with a song on his lips. Later, he called out, 'Aren't you going to give me my insulin, darling?'

Susanna hesitated, then entered the bedroom, accompanied by Maggie, who carried the necessary equipment—a new needle and syringe, and the vial of insulin.

The Signor bared his arm and turned his face away.

Susanna took the syringe from Maggie, but instead of drawing the insulin into it, she drew in a syringe full of air. Gently as ever, she pushed the needle into his flesh and injected a bubble of air.

'Sorry,' she said, as though just realizing her mistake. 'We forgot the insulin.' And she filled the syringe and gave him another jab. Then she and Maggie left the room.

The air-bubble was on its way, moving unsuspectedly and with great rapidity through the veins of the doomed man.

Susanna and Maggie were barely out of the room when they heard an agonized cry. Maggie dropped the tray of vials and syringes. Susanna rushed into the bedroom. The Signor was struggling to get up, his hands clutching his chest. His head was thrown back, as he struggled to breathe. His face and neck began to swell, his chest wall bulged. He coughed once, then pitched forward and brought up blood; then he lay still.

❧

'A massive heart attack,' said Dr Dutta, making out the death certificate. 'Did he suffer from blood pressure?'

'Yes. And diabetes.'

'Had he exerted himself recently?'

'He'd been out riding.' She did not mention the duel with whips. 'His horse fell, and he walked home in the rain.'

'That probably brought it on. Well, you'd better inform his embassy. And take care of yourself, Susanna. You look pale and tired. You've been under some strain, I can see. Give yourself a long rest. And don't get married in a hurry. Your husbands appear to be more of a liability than a support. You're the type who attracts men of weak character. They will fasten on to you as vines fasten themselves to a sturdy, independent tree. You don't need such men. Keep them at bay.'

This conversation was repeated to me by Susanna a few days later, when her household had settled down to its normal routine. Her late husband's body was taken to Delhi, thus depriving Jimmy Rogers and his guitar of a companion in the Meerut cemetery. Signor Romero was shipped off to the Argentine, to be buried near his ancestral home. It is not known if his favourite whip was buried with him.

The Goonga recovered from his ordeal, albeit with only one good eye. He carried on with his duties as though nothing had happened. In fact, he won more races than before, largely because the other jockeys were superstitious about his one fearsome eye, and kept as far away from him as possible.

And did Susanna take the friendly doctor's advice and avoid further matrimony? Time alone would tell . . .

But one day, when I was sitting beside her under the neem trees, and trying to be sympathetic, she surprised me by saying something that was totally unexpected and yet revealing of her inner self.

'I can't help it,' she said. 'I feel the need of a husband, but the more I see of him, the more I hate him. It's the sudden hatred which practically every wife sometimes feels for her husband just because he *is* her husband. It's real hatred. It grows upon you. And I can't help what I'm doing.'

As I walked home, I kept hearing those words of Susanna's. 'I can't help what I'm doing . . .'

EPISODE SIX

the health club

In her thirties Susanna was more beautiful than she had been in her twenties. It wasn't just physical beauty. She seemed to glow all over, give out a certain radiance that attracted men as a bright lamp attracts a variety of insects. The men who succumbed to her charms were very much like insects—no match for the spider who, though often mistaken for an insect, is actually a different and far superior creature.

The trouble was, Susanna did not realize that she was a superior being compared to the creatures with whom she sought alliances. Hence she was doomed to disappointment.

'Men get some happiness, but women don't,' she told me one day. 'Certainly not for long. Sometimes I look back and see that I was happy once. A long time ago.'

'When were you happy?'

'When I was a girl—when I went out riding with my father, when I helped him train the horses, when I followed his fortunes on the racecourse . . .'

'What you need is a father, not a husband,' I said.

'You would make a good father.'

'But I can't be your father. I can only be a younger brother.'

She nodded. 'But you have a fatherly manner. I can confide in you. When I was a girl—dreaming of the sort of man I'd marry—it never occurred to me that all men are alike, that you can pick one off a busy street and he would turn out to be no different from the others. Commonplace . . .'

'So why did you marry them?'

'Everyone dreams of the coming of a prince. But when the prince comes, he too is commonplace.'

'So no woman can be happy?'

'Not for long.'

'Would a child have made a difference?'

'Yes. A child would have made the husband more acceptable.'

'But you would still have eaten him up,' I said, laughing.

'Oh, no. They want to be eaten up. Haven't you noticed?'

∾

It was to be some time before I could notice anything of the kind, because later that year I managed to obtain a scholarship to Oxford, and so two years passed before I saw Susanna again.

She was now forty, looking thirty. And I was thirty, looking forty!

And I wasn't surprised to find that she had another husband on the premises.

At least she called him her husband, although it wasn't clear to me (or anyone else) if she was legally his wife or if they were just living together.

Mr Gupta was a short, rotund man of about fifty. He had greying hair, a sagging chin, and he waddled rather than walked. Perhaps he was the father-figure that Susanna needed.

Mr Gupta was a dietician (although he didn't look it) who believed in organic foods, nature cures, herbal remedies, early morning jogging, cold baths in winter, and daily enemas.

In short, he had turned a large part of the estate into a Health Farm.

Every morning at six, when I looked over my wall, I could see about twenty solid citizens, of various shapes and sizes, jogging around the gardens and the estate. They ranged from the local magistrate and his wife to sundry local businessmen, several overweight housewives, a school principal, and a couple of out-of-shape policemen.

Huffing and puffing, and looking quite miserable, they did two or three rounds of the estate before collapsing on the grass and looking at their waistlines to see if they had got their money's worth in terms of an improvement in their figures. Naturally Mr Gupta charged them for the privilege of running about in the grounds in the pursuit of health and happiness.

He did not run himself, but watched from a distance, shouting words of encouragement to his bedraggled flock.

When they were quite exhausted he would have an attendant pass around glasses of juice made from senna pods, guaranteed to cure constipation in half an hour flat. Before that, however, everyone was put to work in Mr Gupta's organic garden, picking tomatoes or ladies' fingers, washing carrots and beetroots, and feeding liquid compost to the mushrooms.

Mr Gupta was a great believer in mushrooms. According to him, they purified the blood, cured skin diseases, prevented baldness, and improved your sex life. He had turned the basement into a mushroom garden, and spent many happy hours watching his mushrooms grow from spores to lovely rounded edible delicacies.

When the members of the Health Club had finished with their exertions, they were sent home. And they were always in a hurry to get home and to the toilet before the senna cocktail took effect.

If the senna did not cure constipation, there was always the enema—a sinister-looking contraption by which soapy water was squirted into the rectum to 'irrigate' the colon, as Mr Gupta put it.

The enema was usually administered by Maggie, who took great pleasure in chasing nervous old gentlemen and hysterical ladies around the gardens, while she waved the enema-can in the air with obvious enjoyment.

Susanna did not take part in all this frivolity but she put up with it because it kept Mr Gupta occupied and happy and brought him some income—which meant he did not have to dip into their joint account more than once or twice a week.

And what did Susanna's staff think of all this tamasha?

The Goonga, of course, could say nothing. He wore a patch over his bad eye, and his one good eye was expressionless. He got on with his work and took no interest in the proceedings.

Maggie, on the other hand, was fully involved, as Mr Gupta depended upon her to administer fruit juices to the ladies whenever they felt exhausted. She was also an adept at massage, and Mr Gupta charged extra for this. And when he discovered that Maggie had six toes on one foot, he told his following that six toes were a sign that the possessor had miraculous healing powers.

Maggie's massages became instantly popular. A little of her 'touch therapy', and those who felt under the weather were soon on top of the weather, frisking about and saying they felt wonderful. Such are the powers of suggestion—and, of course, a good massage.

And what of my friend Shah Rukh? What was his attitude?

Shah Rukh found it a wonderful source of entertainment. He leant against the garden wall, hands on his hips, grinning at all the well-fed health-conscious citizens doing their best to get rid of the flab they had accumulated.

'First they fatten themselves up at the most expensive restaurants, and then they spend more money in trying to get rid of all that lovely fat.'

Shah Rukh had a philosophical turn of mind. And he did not prevent the Health Club members from creating their own vegetable garden—just as long as he was not expected to do all the hard work.

'They must be crazy,' he told me, as he showed me the mushroom patch in the special shed. 'They grow these things in horse-shit, cow-dung, and all sorts of decaying matter, and then they tell you that they are good for the health! Even the wild ones look healthier.' And to prove his point, he took me to a shady spot near the snake-pit and showed me a patch of brightly-coloured mushrooms.

They certainly looked attractive. Some were red, some purple, some green, some crimson with yellow stripes—nature at her most artistic!

'I wouldn't eat them if I were you,' I said. 'These colourful varieties are usually poisonous.'

'I suppose they make you very sick,' he said.

'Worse than that. They are poisonous enough to kill you. As poisonous as those vipers in the tank. Why don't you clear them away?'

'I was about to do so, but Miss Susanna stopped me. She said they looked beautiful.'

'They are certainly beautiful. But sometimes beauty spells danger.'

'Like our lady Susanna? Her husbands were not very lucky.'

'Let's hope Mr Gupta does better. He seems a harmless sort.'

'He calls himself a doctor. Is he a real doctor?'

'I don't know. But all sorts of people call themselves doctor, or are honoured with the title.'

Well, Dr Gupta became quite popular in the town, and people came to consult him for their various ailments. They found the enema treatment rather drastic, but they went along with eating leaves and grass and mushrooms, and apparently no harm was done.

Susanna fond it all very tiresome and boring. She had grown up on mutton chops and grilled fish and roast lamb and fried chicken, not to mention curried prawns, nargisi koftas and an occasional Irish stew. And now, suddenly, all these delicacies were banned from the dining table, and Susanna was expected to follow Gupta's example and subsist on pulses, paneer, fruit and salads. Finally, even the paneer was banned, Dr Gupta having decided to become a complete vegan—forbidding all animal products such as milk, butter, cheese and eggs. Dr Gupta, an easy-going character in many ways, was fanatical on the subject of food, and made Susanna promise not to touch any of the polluting items that she had been consuming all her life.

Susanna put up with this for some time, as she wanted to please and help her dedicated husband. But at times she felt weak and depressed. Basically, she was missing her proteins.

She was becoming increasingly irritable and discontented, and one day she stopped by at my place and asked me if I would do her a favour.

'Sure,' I said. 'Anything you want, including the moon.'

'Better than the moon,' she said. 'I need a good meal. Will you take me out to lunch?'

Well, I took her to the best restaurant in town, and we dined on a spicy Malabar grilled fish, which went well with a bottle of red wine, and Susanna began to look quite happy and relaxed.

'You need a change,' I told her.

'A change of man or a change of menu? All this health food is wearing me down.'

'A change of place,' I said.

'Yes, I should be living in Kerala or Bengal or Goa, where the fish is wonderful!'

'Maybe I can take you to those places some day, when I'm making some money. We can lie on a beach and live off lobsters and prawns.'

'Wonderful!' She clapped her hands, then let out a sigh. 'And meanwhile I must live on methi and dhania—it's growing all over the compound!'

'And mushrooms,' I added. 'You mustn't forget the mushrooms.'

When Dr Gupta learnt that Susanna had gone out with a young man, and indulged in a meal of 'fish, flesh and fowl', he flew into a rage and his blood pressure went up—so high, that he had to drink three bowls of ginger tea to bring it down again. He had quite a row with Susanna, who took it all very calmly, as she knew he wanted some money for a fruit-canning project. When she brought it up, he calmed down. Also, he remembered that he'd invited some very important citizens over for dinner the following evening, and he wanted to give them an impression of peace and harmony in the household.

The important guests included the chairman of the municipality, a sitting MLA, the district magistrate, Susanna's bank manager, and the local correspondent of a Delhi newspaper. Dr Gupta was hoping for some official backing, financial support and, of course, as much publicity as possible. I was there too, as a special invitee of Susanna's.

Serving at the table were Maggie and a younger girl, a relative of hers, who came over to help on such occasions. The meal had been prepared by Dr Gupta's personal cook, who did not allow any contaminating meat, milk or fish into the kitchen. But in preparing the dishes he took some help from Susanna, Maggie and the girl. The vegetables had been presented by members of the Health Club.

The meal began with mushroom soup, and all who partook of it said it was delicious; but no one asked for a second helping. Only Dr Gupta asked for more, putting it away in noisy gulps and proudly proclaiming that he had grown and nurtured the mushrooms with his own hands.

Rice and various salads and vegetable curries followed, the main item being a mushroom curry decorated with sprigs of dhania, mint and some stuff that looked like seaweed. I refused the mushroom curry.

It had a greenish tinge, and reminded me of the colourful mushrooms and toadstools shown to me by Shah Rukh. Susanna also declined the mushroom curry. So did the district magistrate, saying he'd had his fair share of mushrooms in the soup. The journalist tucked into all the dishes—he was a great believer in free meals. The others took modest helpings of the mushroom curry, concentrating on the other dishes.

We were well into the fruit salad when things started happening.

The journalist suddenly clutched his stomach and said he had to go to the toilet. He rushed down the steps and into the bushes.

Dr Gupta then said he was feeling uneasy too. He got up and went indoors.

The others looked at each other in some bewilderment. None of them looked too happy.

'I must get back to my office,' said the bank manager, and began to get up.

'I, too,' said the municipal councillor; but neither could move from their chairs. Both of them looked rather pale. The MLA said nothing. Suddenly he got up, went behind a potted palm and got sick.

I was feeling perfectly well; but then, I hadn't eaten any mushrooms. Nor had Susanna.

Presently Dr Gupta returned, staggering a little.

'I'm all right now,' he said. 'Must be the blood pressure.' He took his seat; and then, without warning, he slumped forward and lay still, his head supported by a fruit bowl.

The MLA was sitting on the steps, looking very green. The journalist was still in the bushes. I went to see if he needed any help. I found him lying on the grass, moaning and only half-conscious.

I ran back to the house, and found the bank manager trying to take Dr Gupta's pulse. He shook his head, saying, 'I can't feel anything.'

Susanna went to the phone.

'I'll call the city ambulance,' she said.

The councillor took the phone from her. 'They'll be here quicker if I talk to them,' he said, and barked out his orders.

When the ambulance arrived, Dr Gupta and the journalist were carried into it and rushed to the hospital.

Dr Gupta was declared dead on arrival. The journalist was in danger for a couple of days but made a slow recovery. The others swore they wouldn't touch mushrooms again.

Later that week, I took a stroll through the grounds and looked for that little patch of colourful wild mushrooms. But the ground around the tree was bare. Not one mushroom remained.

EPISODE SEVEN

love me, love my mobile

It isn't time that's passing by
It is you and I . . .

And in Susanna's case, it was her husbands who were passing by—and passing out!

Is time the great healer? Nobody missed Dr Gupta except perhaps some of his more devoted Health Club members. Without its leader, the club broke up and dispersed. Nobody missed his predecessors either. But Susanna still missed her father.

I realized this when she showed me around the house and opened up the secret room which was always kept locked.

'People think I have some great treasure in this room,' she said. 'I have always kept it closed because it is very private. In a way, it is a treasure room. It was my father's room, and I have kept it as it was since the day he died. Since I was a little girl, in fact. You're a sensitive young man, and that's why I'm showing it to you. None of my husbands have been into this room. None of my servants, either. That's why there are so many rumours about it. The unseen, the hidden, is always mysterious.'

The room had not been disturbed since the old man had died in it. Of course, Susanna dusted it every week, and changed the counterpane on the bed which had been his last resting place.

An old-fashioned armchair, upholstered in leather, took up one corner of the room, and beside it stood a bookshelf taken up by volumes on horses, racing, hunting, fishing and other outdoor activities. On the walls hung three or four prints of English hunting scenes—horses, hounds and colourfully dressed riders in pursuit of the elusive fox. There was also the head of a long-dead leopard, similar to the mounted trophies on the veranda wall.

In another corner of the room, standing upright in a rack, were a double-barrelled gun and a light rook-rifle.

'You can see he was fond of hunting,' said Susanna.

'And fishing too,' I observed, noting the fishing rod and tackle on the same shelf. 'And was he a swordsman?'

Mounted on the wall were two swords, well polished and well preserved. I examined the blades. They were very sharp, and the steel was free of rust, heavy, capable of inflicting severe wounds.

'They were his father's swords,' said Susanna. 'One is a Maratha sword—it was given to him by one of Shivaji's descendants. The other is an English sword. It was presented to him by the Begum Samru. Or so I was told.'

'Your grandfather knew the begum?'

'He supplied her with the best Deccani horses. That was how my parents met. Mother was a distant relation of the begum's.'

'I have seen the begum's portrait. You do resemble her a bit.' In more ways than one, I might have added.

'Well, these are treasures enough,' I said, as we left the room. 'And that sword—it could slice a man's head off with one clean stroke.'

I could see why Susanna needed a father-figure (not a young stripling like me), and it was obvious that she had been mismatched in her chequered married life. Apparently she had inherited at least one quality of the begum's—a weakness for handsome but somewhat empty-headed men, of whom she had tired rather quickly.

So it did not surprise me when she took up with Mr Sammy

Das, a much older man, who owned a couple of cinemas and a printing press in the city. He must have been some twenty years older than Susanna. He was in his mid-sixties, but very spry, very active, and an attentive and satisfying marital partner. Finally, Susanna had found a husband who was also a father-figure.

As for Sammy, he was very much in love with Susanna, and whenever they were in each other's arms he would say, 'There is nothing I would like better than to die in your arms.'

Prophetic words!

Sammy had seen Susanna for years, admiring her from a distance without making much effort to get to know her better. He had seen her husbands come and go, and did not give any credence to the rumours that she had sped them on their way. Nor did he believe that she was a witch, as some simple souls believed. And when a local newspaper tried to come out with a scandalous piece on Susanna, he refused to print it. The newspaper belonged to someone else, but the press was his, and he told them to take their libellous tale elsewhere.

Sammy Das had only one vice, if you could call it that. He was deeply attached to his cellphone.

A great many people are attached to their cellphones and don't move about without them. But in Sammy's case it was an obsession. It was more than a toy, more than a necessity—it had become a part of him, like an arm or a leg—and he was quite helpless without it.

So, if he was in love with his cellphone, why did he need a wife?

He was a widower with grown-up, married children, and he felt the need of a companion. Also, he was head-over-heels in love with Susanna. He couldn't take his eyes off her (even when talking on his cellphone) and he was at his happiest when she accompanied him on a business trip or attended a premiere at one of his cinemas. She came to the opening night of *Maqbool* and stole the limelight from most of the stars. He was proud to have her on his arm, and his face lit up whenever he heard someone remark, 'Now where did Sammy get that beautiful young wife?'

And Sammy was so attentive and so loving that Susanna became quite fond of him. Only that cellphone was a bit of a nuisance, ringing during meals, ringing when they were out for a walk, ringing while they were watching a film, ringing while he was sitting in the toilet, ringing while they were making love!

Susanna had put up with much worse, but at times she felt like taking the cellphone and throwing it into the snake tank. Except that Sammy would probably jump into the tank to rescue it!

'I do wish you wouldn't keep it under your pillow,' she remonstrated. 'Do you really enjoy being woken up in the middle of the night?'

'It's from the ticket-office, my dear, we had a house-full at the Roxy tonight.'

'But they could have told you that in the morning.'

'They know I'll sleep better when I know the day's receipts.'

And a few minutes later there would be a similar call from the Odeon, informing him of the day's receipts.

'Now that the suspense is over, shall we sleep?'

'Not until I've shown you how much I love you.' And Sammy would proceed to make passionate love to Susanna, reaching a climax just as the phone began to ring again!

'One minute, dear. After this call I'll switch it off.'

But it seemed one of the presses had broken down, and the newspaper's proprietor was threatening to take his business to another press. 'I'll be there in half an hour,' said Sammy. And to Susanna: 'I'll have to go, my dear, the press has broken down.'

'And so will you, if you carry on like this.'

Sammy was a perfectionist. He was a fervent lover, and Susanna had no complaint (other than the cellphone) but he wanted to show her that he was as good a lover as any young man, and possibly even better. So he visited the local chemist and came back with a strip of Viagra tablets.

It was some time before Susanna came to know about the Viagra, and in the meantime Sammy become even more amorous and demanding both in and out of bed. This did not prevent him from attending to his cellphone, even at the most inconvenient times.

He would bury his face between her breasts and utter the most passionate endearments, only to have them broken off by the insistent ringing of the cellphone.

'Darling, who do you love more, me or your mobile?' asked Susanna one day.

'You, of course, my dear. But we can't neglect the business, can we?'

'I don't think your business will suffer if you could switch off that phone for five minutes.'

Dutifully he'd switch it off, but two minutes later he would quietly switch it on again.

'I just can't do without it,' he confessed. 'It has become a part of me—an extra sense, a fourth dimension!'

'And I'm still in the third dimension,' said Susanna. 'One day that phone will give you all the pleasure you want, and even a wife will be superfluous.'

When Susanna found the Viagra tablets on the bathroom shelf, she laughed and said, 'What do you need these for? You're perfectly normal without them.'

'They help me a little,' said Sammy, feeling embarrassed. 'It means that while I'm talking on the phone I can continue making love to you.'

'How insulting!' said Susanna, and she took his cellphone and threw it down the well in the garden.

Of course he got another. And another. Soon the house was full of them.

Susanna hid them whenever she could, but Sammy was like an alcoholic who succeeds in hiding his bottle in the most unlikely places. He hid his cellphones in flowerpots, empty dishes, dressing-gown pockets, even waste-paper baskets. Guests who sat down in easy chairs were sometimes startled by a cellphone ringing beneath the cushion.

'It's a new type of mobile,' joked Sammy. 'You get the message through your bottom.'

Late one evening, after making a round of his cinemas, and press, Sammy came home very tired. Still, he was in an amorous mood, and after dinner he took three Viagra pills instead of just one. 'Bet I can't have just one,' he said, taking a line from an ad for potato chips. He was so amorous and passionate that night, he ignored the ringing of his cellphone.

Susanna thought he had fallen asleep in her arms.

'Your cellphone is ringing,' she said. 'Shall I answer it for you?'

There was no response from Sammy. Susanna put her hand under his pillow and switched off the phone.

'Poor dear,' she said, 'you really are exhausted.'

After a few minutes Susanna noticed that Sammy wasn't breathing. She felt for his pulse. There was no pulse-beat. She switched on the bedside lamp. Sammy's eyes were open but there was no life in them. His wish had come true—he had died in Susanna's arms.

∼

I came over next morning to help Susanna with the funeral arrangements. She had come to depend on me for help in such practical matters. Sammy, like Jimmy Rogers before him, was a Christian, albeit not a very devout one. Nevertheless, he was entitled to a place beside Jimmy in the cemetery.

The coffin was brought to the house, and with some help from Shah Rukh and the Goonga, Sammy was placed in it, now wearing his best suit, for Maggie and her assistant had dressed him up for the occasion.

As we were about to close the coffin, one of Sammy's cellphones began to ring. It was the one he had placed in a flowerpot. Susanna located it and took the call. It was simply a commercial for an after-shave lotion.

'I don't think he'll be needing any,' said Susanna. And then as an afterthought she said, 'He was so fond of his cellphone, why don't we bury one with him?' And she placed the phone in his coat pocket, saying, 'At least he'll have some company for a few hours.'

Quite a crowd had gathered at the cemetery, for Sammy Das was a respected and popular citizen. As the coffin was being lowered into the grave, the cellphone began to ring. All present looked startled; then there were a few smiles. The ringing subsided, and the old priest read out the burial service. Flowers were thrown into the grave. As the mourners began to drift away, the phone began to ring again.

I was standing beside Susanna. 'He's trying to call you,' I said.

'No,' said Susanna. 'He wants to know if the paper has come out on time.'

farewell, susanna

Life on Susanna's estate continued quite placidly. But Susanna decided to sell her horses. Horse racing as a sport was no longer very popular in northern India, and she could not afford to move her stables to Bombay or Calcutta. The syces and the Goonga were pensioned off, and reluctantly the Goonga retired to his village.

By now Susanna had stopped looking for a suitable husband—or so it seemed. I think she had decided that the ideal husband did not—could not—exist.

I, on the other hand, was beginning to think in terms of a suitable wife for myself. My parents had always disapproved of my friendship with a woman who was ten years my senior and who had gone through so many husbands. And whenever I said 'But we are just good friends,' my mother had looked rather doubtful.

'An older woman draws the sap out of a young man,' she had said more than once. 'She takes away his manhood.'

I had protested that my relationship with Susanna was not a physical one—that it was purely platonic. But my mother had said, 'Ah, but you can be affected mentally as well. You will lose your power to think clearly. She is, after all, a Black Widow spider—she preys on men. She would like a young one for a change! Someone like you . . .'

My parents were, therefore, relieved and happy when I told them about Shashibala, who had just done her History

Honours under my tutelage, and with whom I had struck up a friendship in recent months.

Shashi was dark and lovely—a southern belle, and a champion swimmer too. That was where we met—at the University swimming pool, where I took her on in a 100-metre freestyle race—and she beat me by a couple of lengths! It was love at first sight.

Her father was an eminent History professor, with liberal views. My parents were only too happy to approve of the union. We were married at a quiet ceremony in Delhi and went to Goa for our honeymoon. More swimming—and lots of loving!

I hadn't forgotten Susanna. Indeed, I was looking forward to presenting my new bride to her. Shashi had, of course, heard about my fascinating neighbour, and was curious to meet her. All the stories she had heard about the 'Merry Widow' had led her to expect a wicked-looking old lady all dressed in black—a veritable witch!

On our second day back in Meerut, I looked over the wall, expecting to see Shah Rukh or even Susanna, but it was the Goonga standing in the driveway, making faces at me!

Shah Rukh explained. 'He got tired of living in his village and the village got tired of him. He was always a little cracked, you know—and he kept getting worse, doing crazy things like keeping snakes for pets, talking to cows and donkeys and even teasing the village girls. Finally, the villagers chased him away, and here he is, back with us. Miss Susanna has made him her messenger, but he doesn't deliver any messages. He just wanders about the town and spends his money on gulab-jamuns.'

'No better way to enjoy one's retirement,' I remarked, as the Goonga strolled away, whistling. He could whistle even if he couldn't talk.

༄

I took my young wife to meet Susanna.

Susanna had been invited to the wedding, but she hadn't come. She hadn't even sent a present. That seemed strange to me. It was unlike her.

Her attitude, when I presented Shashi, was stranger still. She seemed positively hostile. Never before had I encountered jealousy in a woman like Susanna. I hadn't realized that she felt so possessive of me. Of course, we had been friends for years, and I think she felt that she was losing me in some way. I had been a companion in a way that her husbands had never been.

She was very polite to Shashi, but I could see there was no warmth in her greeting.

'Well, I hope you will be very happy together,' she said. 'You must let me know if you need anything.'

'All we need is your blessing,' said Shashi.

Susanna smiled at her, but the smile was not in her eyes. And she did not look at me at all.

She did not ask me to visit her, and whenever I passed her on the road or met her at the club, she was remote, even cold towards me. How could I have guessed that beneath her indifferent exterior there simmered unfulfilled desires and a frustrated passion that was fast turning into resentment against me and mine. In an imperfect world, love soon turns to hate. And the female of the species is more deadly than the male.

When the Goonga left a basket on our veranda, salaamed quickly, and walked off with a swagger, I thought Susanna had relented and sent me a basket of guavas—for old times' sake.

'Has she sent me a present?' asked Shashi innocently; for she did not know much about Susanna or her history.

'Must be some fruit,' I said. 'Take a look.'

Shashi removed the lid from the basket and exclaimed, 'Oh, mushrooms! I love mushrooms!'

I got up from my easy chair and took a look at the mushrooms. They looked innocent enough.

'Yes, she grows mushrooms,' I said. 'But at this time of the year—the end of the rains—the poisonous type sometimes get mixed up with the good ones. Better not eat them.'

'Oh, I'm sure they'll be all right,' said Shashi. 'They look perfectly all right.'

I took the basket from her. 'You mustn't take any chances,' I said. And I emptied the basket into the garbage can.

'Oh, you've thrown them all away,' she cried. 'She'll feel terribly insulted!'

'Well, we won't tell her,' I said. 'We'll say they were just fine.'

Shashi was upset and did not talk to me for several hours. It was our first quarrel! But she was never angry for long, and that same evening she made my favourite halwa, and after dinner we went for a walk along the Mall Road. Diwali was approaching, and the night air was cool and balmy. On our way home, Susanna drove past me, but she did not stop. Perhaps she had not seen us; or maybe she was in a hurry.

A few days later, as we were about to sit down for breakfast, Shashi looked out of the window and exclaimed: 'Oh look, another basket! More mushrooms, I suppose.'

'I doubt it,' I said. 'We didn't thank her for the last lot.'

But I joined her on the veranda, and together we inspected the basket. Impulsively, Shashi stooped and removed the cover.

'Guavas!' she exclaimed. 'How nice of her. And look, here's a card. It says: "To remind you of old times . . ." What does that mean?'

'Nothing much. When I was a boy, I used to climb her guava trees and pinch the guavas. That was how I first met her.'

'Well, let me try one,' said Shashi and selected a juicy-looking guava. I took one too. And then, as Shashi lifted the basket, a black snake—a four-foot-long viper—emerged from beneath the top layer of guavas, uncoiled itself, and raised its head to strike.

I knocked the basket from Shashi's hands. The guavas rolled down the steps. The snake fell too, and glided away. Another viper fell out of the basket, and the pair of them wriggled away across the path and disappeared into the bushes.

I caught Shashi as she fainted. Picking her up, I carried her indoors. When she recovered, she said, 'And what was all that about? To remind you of old times?'

'I don't know,' I said. 'But I'll find out.'

❧

Later that morning, I confronted Susanna on her veranda.

'What do you mean by sending us that basket of guavas with two vipers hidden amongst them?'

Susanna was taken aback. 'I never sent any guavas.'

'Well, somebody tried to kill us. Thank you for the fruit—but no thanks for the snakes!'

'I would do nothing to harm you. Surely you know that.' She looked up at me with the old affection in her eyes. 'You do believe me?'

'And my wife? Why should anyone want to harm her?'

'No one that I know of—'

But she paused, and seemed lost in thought. 'The Goonga—he's going quite mad—and only he could have handled those snakes.'

'If it was Goonga, he'll have to go.'

And the Goonga went. He simply disappeared. Some said he'd gone back to his village. Some said he was in a lunatic asylum. Some said he had drowned himself in the Ganga canal. Susanna had no idea of his whereabouts. He had simply gone away, never to be seen again.

❧

We were invited to dinner.

Susanna was desperate to hold on to my friendship, and she went out of her way to be nice to Shashi.

It was the evening of Diwali, and no sooner had dusk fallen than the air was crackling with fireworks, the sky alight with rockets. While we sat down to dinner, Shah Rukh was busy on the veranda steps, letting off a variety of fireworks—crackers, fountains, sparklers, rockets. It was hard to believe that Susanna was facing financial difficulties. She appeared to have emptied her bank account in order to have a good Diwali.

It was a candlelit dinner, partly out of choice and partly due to a power failure which lasted for some time.

Susanna and Maggie had together prepared a sumptuous dinner—all the things I liked: koftas, kebabs, biryani, bitter gourds . . . No mushrooms! There was nothing suspicious about the meal, although Shashi ate very little; she was a little apprehensive. The stuffed gourds did taste rather strange, and I could not finish mine.

Everyone was in a good mood—until a storm broke outside. A sudden gust of wind blew out the candle. Maggie rushed off to find a kerosene lamp. A roll of thunder was followed by flashes of lightning. It started raining, and Shah Rukh had to put an end to his fireworks display.

It was then that Shashi started complaining about feeling unwell. She was feeling giddy, she said, and felt like throwing up.

It may have been the food, or it may have been psychological, but she was definitely in some discomfort.

'I'll take you home,' I said, and supporting her, I walked her home in the light rain that was beginning to fall.

After I had put her to bed, I looked out of the window and was surprised to see Susanna's house lit up in a blaze of light. Had Shah Rukh started a bonfire or had a corner of the house been struck by lightning?

'What's wrong?' asked Shashi from her bed.

'I don't know. There seems to be a fire at the house.'

'You'd better go and see.'

'Will you be all right on your own?'

'Yes, I'm feeling better now.'

As I watched from the window, the fire seemed to have spread. One end of the old house was ablaze.

As I stepped out on the veranda, I saw someone running out of Susanna's front gate. I couldn't be sure, but in the distance it looked like the Goonga.

'What's he doing here?' I wondered. 'I thought he'd run off weeks ago.'

There was no time to go after him. Shah Rukh was running towards me.

'Phone for the fire brigade!' he called. 'Our line is down.'

My line was down too. So was the battery of my mobile phone.

We watched helplessly as the fire spread through the house.

'Where's Susanna?' I asked.

'She ran into her father's room to save some of his things. Maggie is with her.'

'We'd better get them out before they are trapped inside.'

Shah Rukh and I ran back to the burning house, shouting for Susanna and Maggie to come out.

They did not appear.

The storm wind had helped the fire to spread rapidly, and the entire house was ablaze.

'Susanna, Susanna!' we called, but there was no answer.

By daybreak there was nothing left of the building except a few blackened walls and twisted iron fixtures. We found one charred body. It was unrecognizable. But from the gold bracelet still on one wrist we knew it to be Susanna's.

∾

There were just a few people at the funeral, for Susanna's circle of friends had been a limited one. She was buried beside two of her husbands, Jimmy Rogers the pop singer, and Sammy Das the entrepreneur. Beyond them were the graves of the Begum Samru's paramours.

It's hard to decide my feelings as I saw that coffin being

lowered into its grave. The loss of a lifetime's friend is always hard to bear. But was Susanna more than a friend? Had our attachment grown to a point where we had become closely related—not as marriage partners, not as lovers, but as two people bonded together by shared experiences. I had, in a way, been the sharer of all her secrets. An ideal husband. Now there were no more secrets, no more bonding. An emptiness stretched before me.

And that evening the roads too were empty, as the first winter rains swept across the city. I wandered down familiar roads, beset by memories—Susanna in her youth, Susanna in her maturity; Susanna looking up at me in the guava tree, laughing; holding my hand; taking me for a drive along the Ganga canal . . . So many memories, covering so many years . . . They passed before my eyes in rapid succession.

And now I was at her gate, and her car was standing there. Because of the rain, I could not make out who was driving it.

The front door opened, and stepping out into the light from the street lamp was Susanna.

At first I thought I was seeing a ghost. I stepped back. And she stepped forward and took my hand. Hers was a warm and living hand.

'I was at your funeral this morning,' I said.

'I know. But that was Maggie. It was she who died in the fire.'

'But your bracelet—?'

'I had given it to her the day before. I had already decided to leave.'

'And where were you when the house burnt down?'

'I was in the Naag Temple. I had kept some jewellery there. All that I had left. But enough for me, now that I'm going away.'

'Why must you leave?'

'Because too much has happened here. Too much unhappiness.'

'But you were happy sometimes.'

'Only when I wasn't looking for happiness. All those men I married . . . Imperfect beings, all of them.'

'None of us is perfect.'

'True. But we can aim for perfection. You came closer to it than anyone else. You were always there beside me when I needed you. Better than a husband. Perhaps, even now . . .'

There was a pause.

'There are no imperfect horses,' I said. 'Only imperfect men.'

'And imperfect women. I was always looking for the right person in the wrong place.'

'Where are you going now?'

'Far away, where no one knows me.

'Well, I hope you do find the right person, wherever it is you're going.'

'I'm not looking for the right person.'

I shrugged. 'You never know.'

'Bye, Arun. I'll write to you.'

We stood there in the lamplight for several minutes, just touching each other, whispering our goodbyes. Had I been older, had she been younger, things might have worked out differently. And if they had, I wondered, would I have become Husband Number Seven? Or had I been that all along?

'Well, here's looking at you,' she said, with her familiar, slightly wicked smile.

Then she got into her car and drove away.

∾

The swords were at my place—a parting gift.

I did not see Susanna again. I'm still waiting to hear from her. I wonder if she married once more. Who knows? Perhaps the number seven would prove lucky for her.

Sometimes I visit that grave in the cemetery, which is supposed to be hers. Her name is inscribed on the tombstone.

I have even placed flowers on the grave, knowing full well that she is not there. Never mind, the flowers are for Maggie as well. She provides a link with the living Susanna.

I must be the only person who knows that the occupant of the grave is not Susanna.

Gravestones don't always tell the true story.

7 KHOON MAAF

A screenplay by
Vishal Bhardwaj and Matthew Robbins

Based on Ruskin Bond's *Susanna's Seven Husbands*

7 ख़ून माफ़

Int. Office. Day.

On top of a neatly organized office table, next to a couple of Buddha idols, lies a jet black revolver. A few moments pass . . . We see a hand casually approach the weapon and pick it up.

We see a lady place the barrel of a gun to her temple. We will come to know her as Susanna Anna-Marie Johannes, 53–54. She has a grim expression as tears flow down her face.

Hesitating for a brief moment, she pulls the gun away . . .

Then within moments, the barrel is placed back to her temple, and this time she has made up her mind. She slowly begins to squeeze the trigger, each micro-second tormenting her. The vibrations of the chamber revolving ever so slowly send waves of fear through her skull.

Suddenly BANG!!!

We see blood splatter on a wall. It slowly begins to flow downward as music creeps in.

Fade to:

The title of the film—7 ख़ून माफ़

Fade in:

Int. Forensic laboratory. Day.

Tracking shot. A steel box placed on a rolling cart is pushed by a technician down a series of spotless corridors in a high-tech research centre in Mumbai.

Int. Private office. Day.

The box arrives at the office of a senior researcher who's bent over a microscope and surrounded by chemical test equipment.

He glances up at the technician, then signs a receipt for the box.

It's Arun, very official here in a lab coat and name tag. As the technician exits, he reads the tag attached to the box.

He freezes at what he sees.

Insert.

The tag reads: SUSANNA JOHANNES.

Int. Conference room. Day.

At the head of the conference table, the Department Head, with a cop besides him, flicks through a stack of documents while addressing Arun and another lab official.

Arun is seated. His face is pale but impassive.

DEPARTMENT HEAD. Susanna Anna-Marie Johannes—छह शादियाँ, और छहें पति, स्वर्गलोक . . .

COP. She must've been one hell of a lay . . .

The lab official lets out a snicker. Arun tries to suppress his emotions.

DEPARTMENT HEAD. पूरे घर के साथ, खुद को राख कर

दिया . . . Suicide . . . Recovery—some bones and ashes. DNA profiling करना है. Dr Kumar, कितने मसरूफ़ हैं आप ?

ARUN. जी, I'll do it.

DEPARTMENT HEAD. Her make-up kit and hair brush . . . Priority case है, police wants to be sure that she's dead.

Arun looks at the box.

Cut to:

Int. Arun's bedroom—Mumbai. Night.

Nandini, Arun's wife, wakes up and realizes that Arun's not in bed by her side.

Int. Arun's kitchen. Night.

Arun's on a step ladder, rummaging in a cupboard above the refrigerator. He brings out a dusty carton, wipes down the lid and opens the carton.

He lifts out a stack of dog-eared binders and spiral-bound workbooks. They're covered in colourful, boyish scribbles.

Nandini walks up from behind him, watching as he goes through the carton.

Under a tattered football jersey, Nandini spots a framed class photo of Arun at age 14 in a white shirt and tie. Meanwhile, Arun produces a bulging photo album.

Opening the album, Nandini points out a picture of Susanna, standing with some party-goers in 1982. She is young, vivacious and stunning.

NANDINI. ये है न . . . Susanna . . .?

Arun speaks with a heavy lump in his throat.

ARUN. 'साहेब' . . . हैं नहीं . . . थीं . . .!

Arun is holding back tears, as Nandini takes his hand. The camera moves to the photo album.

Dissolve to:

Super—आदमख़ोर मेजर

Ext. Stables. Day.

The year is 1978.

ARUN (*voice-over*). ज़िंदगी से लबालब और इश्क़ में मायूस मेरी उदास उदास साहेब। तमाम उम्र सच्चे प्यार की तलाश में ख़ानाबदोश रहीं। बोहत अकेली थीं साहेब। पैदाइश पे माँ गुज़र गयीं और होश संभाला तो पिता, बड़े साहेब, सब थे उनके—दोस्त, माँ, बाबा, भाई। उनके जाने के बाद जाने-अनजाने हर आदमी में वो उन्हीं को तलाशा करती थीं . . .

Four ragamuffin farm boys are dragging bales of hay from an ox cart into a stable well stocked with thoroughbreds. The boys' bare feet and clothes are caked with mud.

A graying dwarf stands on an overturned bucket, issuing orders. Deaf since birth, he's known as Goonga. His speech— no more than guttural locutions—is incomprehensible, but the boys follow his instructions well enough.

The scrawniest of the kids, pausing to rest for a moment, winces as the Goonga jabbers his name and whacks him on the butt with a riding crop.

As the lad scampers back to work, it becomes clear that . . . it's Arun, age 8–9.

ARUN (*voice-over*). गूंगा चाचा, कहने को तो गूंगा था, पर बोलता बहुत था। मैं तो पैदा ही अनाथ हुआ। उसने गोद में तो कभी नहीं लिया, पर सब कहते थे कि उसने मुझे गोद ले लिया।

A tall, handsome Army officer pulls up in an open top Land Rover. He's accompanied by an immaculately dressed servant, Ghalib, who leaps out and holds open the car door.

The officer steps out, taking care to keep his polished boots clean and dry. This is Captain Edwin Rodriques, 35–37, a conspicuously dashing marksman and athlete.

The boys stop and stare; other stable hands appear in the doorway, smiling uncertainly.

The Captain is not pleased. He points at Goonga.

RODRIQUES. You . . . गूंगा . . .

He shows him his watch.

RODRIQUES. और कितना time लगेगा . . .?

Goonga responds with some garbled barks. Rodriques turns to Ghalib.

RODRIQUES. ग़ालिब . . . what the devil is he saying?

Ghalib points at the kids and gestures to Goonga to lock them inside after the work is done.

ARUN (*voice-over*). ग़ालिब भाई, नाम से शायर काम से butler और दिल से हिन्दी फिल्मों के villain . . .

GHALIB. Sir ये कहना चाह रहा है कि आधे घंटे में सब चकाचक हो जाएगा . . .

RODRIQUES. Hmmm . . . उससे कहो कि एक भी पिल्ला बाहर नहीं दिखना चाहिए . . .

Goonga steps off the bucket and walks towards Ghalib, muttering something in a cheeky tone. Ghalib hides his expression and turns to the Captain.

GHALIB. और कुछ Sir . . .?

The Captain looks at Goonga, who looks back at him with contempt in his eyes.

RODRIQUES. क्या बोला इसने . . .?

Ghalib tries to smile.

GHALIB. शुक्रिया . . . Thank you.

Rodriques studies Goonga for a few moments and looks at Ghalib whose smile broadens. He nods and turns back to walk towards his jeep. Ghalib turns to Goonga and speaks in a hushed tone.

GHALIB. गूंगे . . . उसे चूतिया बोल रहा है . . . साले, पता चल गया तो आँखे निकाल लेगा तेरी . . .

Goonga hits his fist into his palm, making a lewd gesture. Ghalib turns back and runs behind the jeep.
  Visible on a hill behind the house is a stone chapel, its steeple jutting skyward.
  Pre-lap: the tolling of the church bell.

Cut to:

Ext. Chapel. Day.

A hundred mourners stand on the flagstone walkway outside the chapel as the bell clangs. Goonga and Ghalib are lined up off to the side with the other servants, all of them neatly dressed.

Pallbearers carry a casket to a hearse waiting outside. The local priest follows, then an altar boy carrying a framed portrait of the deceased. Then, the Captain appears, looking appropriately solemn.

Leaning on the Captain's arm is a slender woman clad in black silk. Her face is hidden behind a mourning veil.

ARUN (*voice-over*). उस दिन काले लिबास के अंदर से वो ऐसे बरस रहीं थीं जैसे पहाड़ों पे रात में चुपचाप बर्फ़ बरसा करती है . . . काला रंग उनपे बहुत फबता था और वक़्त के साथ वो रंग उनका रंग बन गया . . .

The camera moves to a nearby tree. Arun is concealed in the foliage, gawking at the mysterious woman. Goonga is glaring at him. But Arun doesn't care: he's in heaven.

Ext. Riding ring. Day.

Susanna's in the saddle, riding a gleaming thoroughbred around the ring. Her hair is pinned up under a riding cap; she's wearing a snug-fitting hacking jacket and jodhpurs.

The Captain stands in the centre of the ring, guiding the horse by means of a lunge line.

The stable boys are mucking out the stalls. Lingering in the doorway, Arun can't keep his eyes off Susanna, who has cast off the rope. Susanna playfully snatches the Captain's cap. Laughing, he tries to retrieve it, but she deftly guides her horse out of reach.

When he bellows in protest, she spurs the horse.

ARUN (*voice-over*). उन दिनों वो मेरी देवी थीं और मैं उनका प्रेम पुजारी . . .

Int. Arun's quarters. Same.

Arun stands in front of a framed picture of a god, raising a couple of burning incense sticks and worshiping the deity.

Looking back to see that nobody is around, he reaches out to the picture frame and pulls out a photo of Susanna and worships her picture with the incense, and places it back behind.

Ext. Naag Temple. Day.

Arun stands in an overgrown part of the estate, on the rocky edge of a dark pool of water thirty feet below. There, among the floating lotus leaves, a dozen snakes are gliding in lazy circles.

ARUN (*voice-over*). साहेब की तिकड़ी का तीसरा इक्का, Maggie aunty, जिनकी गोद मे साहेब बड़ी हुई थीं। माँ भी थीं और सहेली भी।

Susanna appears, followed by Maggie, 48, a grumpy but devoted house servant who carries a tray with a pitcher of milk.
   Susanna goes down a rough-hewn flight of steps, and by means of a pulley and plank, little Arun carefully lowers the pitcher to her.

ARUN (*voice-over*). वैसे और भी कई दोस्त थे साहेब के थोड़े ज़हरीले, थोड़े ख़तरनाक, मगर उनके पूरे वफ़ादार।

Susanna, who is now walking slowly amid a colony of hissing, swaying snakes! They make way for her as she puts some milk into saucers all over the grotto floor.

Int. Solarium. Day.

Now young Arun's in spotless, starched white cotton livery. His face has been scrubbed and his hair slicked down. He follows Goonga, who is equally immaculate, into a solarium, each of them carrying a silver platter piled high with petits-fours.
   In the sun-filled room, Susanna is holding court with the Captain and half a dozen wealthy horse owners. Various

fawning servants see to the serving of the finest Coorg coffee.

RODRIQUES. It's a derby, darling. The jockey is as important as our stallion.

SUSANNA. I see no reason to change anything, Rod. गूंगा daddy का favourite jockey रहा है . . .

The Captain looks at Goonga with contempt.

RODRIQUES. Hmm . . .! What do you think, Martha . . .?

The lady pushes a wad of cake into her mouth as he speaks.

MARTHA. I am sure someone here can come up with a better idea.

A portly horse owner, Mr Rangan, smiles at Susanna.

RANGAN. हम बाहर से कोई professional rider hire क्यों नहीं करते . . .? We can afford it and I know one in Prague.

Susanna, who is lost in her thoughts, notices Arun stealthily making his way past everyone present towards the coffee tray and putting sugar cubes into his pockets.

SUSANNA. You . . . boy . . . क्या कर रहे हो वहाँ . . .?

Arun sharply turns to face her and speaks almost immediately.

ARUN. चोरी . . .

There is a giggle among the people. Susanna also smiles.

SUSANNA. Come here . . .

Arun walks up to her. Goonga is shocked. He tries to move ahead but Ghalib stops him.

SUSANNA. हाथ निकालो बाहर . . .

Arun brings out his fists full of sugar cubes. The Captain looks around

RODRIQUES. किसका पिल्ला है ये . . .?

Arun turns to the Captain.

ARUN. ये Candy के लिए चुरायी है मैंने . . .

SUSANNA. Who's Candy?

Arun turns from the Captain to Susanna.

ARUN. आपका नया घोड़ा . . .

SUSANNA. Oh! That's a nice name for him. Candy . . .

This gives Arun a little courage to speak his mind.

ARUN. He run fast when he eat it.

Susanna softly laughs.

SUSANNA. कहाँ तक पढ़े हो . . .?

ARUN. Seven and half.

Another giggle.

SUSANNA. और कुछ कहना चाहते हो . . .

Arun straightens up.

ARUN. Yes, साहेब . . . Candy loves you. You tik-tok him in race and win *debry.*

There is an awkward silence amongst the guests for a brief moment, and then they break into laughter. The Captain is not amused.

RODRIQUES. What the fuck . . .

Goonga, muttering gibberish, pulls Arun by his collar and drags him out of the room as Susanna laughs.

Cut to:

Int. Stables. Day.

Goonga is jabbering an angry tirade as he chases Arun through the stables, whipping his long leather hunter. It's a long chase and finally Arun collides with someone and falls to the ground.

It's Susanna, accompanied by Ghalib. Goonga stops and bows down as Arun hides behind her.

Goonga, in his usual guttural fashion, tries to apologize as Ghalib translates it simultaneously.

GHALIB. Miss साहेब . . . माफ़ी . . . अनाथ समझ के दया की मैंने, मैं इस हरामज़ादे को गाँव वापस भेज रहा हूँ . . . ये कल से काम पे नहीं आएगा . . .

Goonga nods, giving his reassurance to what Ghalib speaks.

SUSANNA. Right . . . ये कल से काम पे नहीं आएगा क्यूँकि . . . ये कल से स्कूल जाएगा . . .

She looks at Arun and smiles.

SUSANNA. Okay . . . Sugar . . .?

Arun smiles back.

ARUN. साहेब . . . Thank you . . .

Susanna leaves Goonga shocked. Arun walks to him, takes the hunter from his hand, and whips it in the air, making a cracking sound.
Cut to:

Int. School. Day.

Arun, neatly dressed and carrying a schoolbag, stands in the doorway of a classroom. The well-bred and well-fed students swivel in their desks to scrutinize him.

ARUN (*voice-over*). शटाक! . . . एक फटके में मेरी ज़िंदगी पलट गयी, पलक झपकते ही साहेब ने मुझे कूड़े के ढेर से उठा के फूलदान में लगा दिया . . .

Ghalib whispers in Arun's ear, nudging him forward.

GHALIB. नाम बोल . . .

Arun speaks out uncomfortably.

ARUN. Arun Kumar.

There is a giggle among the students. The teacher, a kind-looking older man, walks up to him.

TEACHER. Come in, Arun, and sit down.

Arun enters and sits on the floor. The other students laugh.

Cut to:

Ext. Race track. Day.

A dozen thoroughbreds thunder around the far turn at the Mysore race track; in the stands, a cheering crowd urges them on.

As one particular stallion flashes over the finish line, Goonga and Arun pound the rail in excitement. Victory! The dwarf and the boy jump up and down, sharing an embrace.

Ext. Winner's circle. Day.

The Captain seizes the reins of the winning mount and helps the jockey to the ground. It's Susanna.

She removes her helmet and waves to the celebrating crowd as some officials place a floral wreath over the horse's neck.

Then she plucks one of the flowers and tosses it to Arun, who catches it and grins with pride.

Int. Solarium. Night.

Still celebrating, Susanna puts a 33 1/3 record on the turntable and takes the Captain in her arms. Counting out the rhythm, she tries to teach him how to waltz.

After a few faltering steps, he gathers her up in his arms and spins her, shrieking with laughter, around the room.

Int. Hut. Night.

In Goonga's hut behind the stable, Arun is hunched over a table which is piled high with school books. By the light of a lantern, he is writing slowly and steadily.

The door bangs open and the dwarf enters, throwing down an armload of tack. He clumps over to the desk and peers, uncomprehending, over Arun's shoulder. The boy never looks up.

Insert: School notebook.

Arun is filling line after line of his copy book with neat, cursive handwriting: 'SUSANNA, SUSANNA, SUSANNA, SUSANNA . . .'

ARUN (*voice-over*). वो मेरी देवी थीं . . . ओर मैं उनका प्रेम पुजारी . . .

Ext. Driveway. Day.

Arun is running full tilt down the driveway toward the stables. He screeches to a halt at the sight of a horse and buggy coming from the house.
    Goonga has the reins; seated behind him are Susanna and the Captain. Susanna signals for a stop.

SUSANNA. Hey Sugar, look at you in such a big hurry. तुम्हें तो school में होना चाहिए इस वक़्त।

ARUN. जी साहेब। पर वो संजय गाँधी के doctor आ रहे थे ना school में तो हम भाग गए।

SUSANNA. क्यूँ?

ARUN. वो सब बच्चों की नसबन्दी कर रहे हैं।

Arun's voice trails off as Susanna laughs out loud.

SUSANNA. Rod! Do you recognize this boy . . .?

The Captain tries to remember him.
    Arun moves forward offering his hand, while mustering his best adult manners.

ARUN. I am Arun Kumar, sir. St Mary's Boys' School, Class 8-B, Roll no. 36 . . . sir.

The Captain is amused by his formal introduction. He shakes Arun's hand.

RODRIQUES. Pleased to meet you, Mr Kumar. This is Captain Rodriques, 1, Para's. (*Turns towards Susanna.*) And this will soon be Mrs Rodriques.

The Captain cuddles the giggling Susanna. Goonga's head snaps around; he is astonished and appalled. Arun, too, is dumbfounded. Goonga harshly whips the horse and the buggy lurches forward. Arun stands alone in the road, watching the waving Susanna as she recedes from view.

Cut to:

Ext. Campfire. Night.

The three servants—Maggie, Ghalib and Goonga, are clustered around the campfire, drinking beer and snacking. The mood is glum.
   Goonga growls an elaborate, gobbledygook complaint.

MAGGIE. No, no, no . . . He is not just a चूतिया. Bastard भी है साला . . . Deadly combination . . . A bastard चूतिया . . .

Goonga growls again and spits more gibberish. Maggie looks at Ghalib, who gulps his drink and smiles.

GHALIB. ज़रूर सुनेंगी Miss साहेब हमारी . . . अभी वो मस्तानी हुई रखी हैं उसके इश्क़ में . . . ना सुन सकती हैं, ना देख सकती हैं . . .

He hands over a drink to Goonga.

GHALIB. जैसे तू . . . कब से पागल भँवरे की तरह बौराता घूम रहा है Maggie की मोहब्बत में . . .

Goonga blushes as Maggie laughs and punches Ghalib.

GHALIB. किसी दिन ग़लती से उसकी skirt गिर गयी तुझपे तो सारी उ
मर रास्ता ढूँढता रहेगा बाहर आने का . . .

Maggie gives Goonga a peck on his cheek.

MAGGIE. हमारी मोहब्बत से कितना जलता है तू . . . मदन पुरी . . .

*Arun, who had come with a plate of peanuts, takes advantage
of the conversation and puts a beer can stealthily into his
pocket.*
*Goonga holds his fist in his palm, making a lewd gesture
towards Ghalib.*
Cut to:

Ext. Campfire. Later.

*Arun stares teary eyed into the glare of the flames. Gulping
down the last of the beer, he hauls out a sheet of paper—his
elaborate 'SUSANNA' note—and rips it up. Tearing it into
shreds he cries as he throws the pieces of paper into the
fire.*

ARUN. I hate you साहेब!

Fade out.

Int. Corridor. Day.

*The present day. Arun walks down various corridors of the
forensic laboratory. Close behind him, a technician rolls a cart
on which sits the steel box full of bones and ashes.*

Int. Office. Day.

*The Department Head leafs through a stack of lab reports
as Arun stands before him,*
On the desk, the steel box.
*The Department Head turns towards the cop from the
previous scene.*

DEPARTMENT HEAD. The samples match. She is dead, then?

The cop looks towards Arun.

COP. Sure, Doc . . . ?

ARUN. Sir . . . हिंदुस्तान के मर्द अब चैन की साँस ले सकते हैं . . .
Cut to:

Int. Arun's Apartment. Night.

Arun is seated at the dining room table, spooning dal and rice into the mouth of a tiny old man whose white hair frames a dark and weathered face.
It's Goonga, bent-over and blind now. He wears an eye patch; his other eye is clouded with a milky cataract.
Nandini studies the photo album as little Aditya sprawls on a rug in the background, doing his homework.

NANDINI. जो भी कहो यार Arun . . . Rodriques था बड़ा handsome.
A dashing fellow.

Arun smiles.

ARUN. Yeah . . . एक सच्चे भारतीय पति के सारे गुण थे उसमें insecure, possessive, boring and महाशक्की . . .

Nandini smiles back.

NANDINI. And a fart king too? Paddu raam . . .

They laugh.
Cut to:

Int. Officers' Club. Night.

It's 1984.

A glamorous reception for Army officers and their wives is underway in the ballroom of the Officers' Club.

The senior officer of the district, Brigadier Venkatesan, addresses the crowd.

He displays his glass of Scotch whisky, full to the brim. All over the ballroom, the happy assemblage follows suit. The Brigadier turns to face Rodriques, who stands modestly to one side, arm in arm with a radiant Susanna.

BRIGADIER. Here's to our very own Major Edwin Rodriques. The winner of the 'Kirti Chakra'. May I speak on the behalf of our brigade, Major, We salute the bravery and courage you displayed during Operation Blue Star. It took a heavy toll on your regiment and, in particular, your company.

RODRIQUES. And my leg!

The Brigadier laughs as the Major waves a walking stick up in the air.

Cut to:

Int. Ballroom. Later.

Couples whirl around the dance floor. The Brigadier chats with the Major in a corner, as a waiter comes up with their drinks on a tray.

The Brigadier nods while taking the glasses, handing one to the Major and taking one for himself.

BRIGADIER. Even the Defence Minister wants to meet you when he comes next month.

He takes the glass of red wine from the tray and offers it to Susanna, who holds the Major's arm and looks completely bored and uninterested.

BRIGADIER. Here, for your beautiful half.

RODRIQUES. She's quit . . . drinking.

BRIGADIER. कब . . .?

Susanna takes the wine glass from him.

SUSANNA. कल . . . मैं रोज़ सुबह पीना छोड़ देती हूँ . . .

The Brigadier joins her in laughter as the Major tries to hide his disdain. A young Lieutenant who looks a little tipsy arrives.

LIEUTENANT. Can I have the pleasure of a dance with the lady . . .?

Susanna looks at the Major who shrugs his shoulders.

RODRIQUES. I had two left feet—lost one . . .

More laughter.
Cut to:

Int. Ballroom. Later.

Susanna is the belle of the ball, dancing with the young lieutenant. Both the dancers are drenched in sweat—it looks as if they have been dancing for a long time, refusing to stop nonetheless. People clap and cheer as the glowering Major watches from the sidelines, gulping down another glass of Scotch.

Int. Men's room. Later.

The Major splashes cold water on his face. Looking up, he sees the handsome Lieutenant and some of his boisterous friends entering.

RODRIQUES. You are quite the dancer, Lieutenant.

The Lieutenant straightens up.

LIUTENANT. Sir . . . but no match to your beautiful
half, sir . . .

*A giggle from his friends. The Major also smiles. The toilet
attendant scurries over to offer the Major a towel. The Major
ignores him as dripping water falls from his face. He limps
over to the other man. Sudden silence.*

RODRIQUES. Beautiful half? Hmm . . . and the better
one too.

*The Lieutenant keeps mum, sensing trouble. The Major walks
up to him and whispers.*

RODRIQUES She has a beautiful name as well
. . . Susanna . . .

The Lieutenant is quiet.

RODRIQUES. What . . .?

LIUTENANT. Susanna.

*WHAM! He smashes his walking stick into his knee. As
the young man crumples, the Major lifts him up and hurls
him, face first, into the mirror. CRASH! He turns and picks
up his stick, takes a few steps, then stops.*

RODRIQUES. You may call her Mrs Rodriques, if you
please.

He exits, his boots crunching on the shards of glass.

Int. Bedroom. Later.

Susanna sits on the side of the bed, looking down and crying like a child. The Major walks restlessly in front of her, holding his stick in one hand and a whisky glass in other.

RODRIQUES. You know you can't handle the fucking alcohol . . . रोज़ सुबह छोड़ देती हूँ . . .

He holds her by the chin.

RODRIQUES. तितली बनना बंद करो अब . . . You are a married woman . . . Are you ashamed to be my wife . . .?

She shakes her head, tears rolling down her cheeks.

SUSANNA. No . . .

RODRIQUES. Then why . . .? क्यूँ मुझे बार-बार यह एहसास दिलाती हो कि मैं लंगड़ा हूँ . . .

She keeps crying and speaks in a choked voice.

SUSANNA. I am sorry . . .

He looks at her for a while and then sits down opposite her. He puts his wooden leg on her lap. She starts to unbuckle it.

RODRIQUES. घर में बच्चे का आना बहोत जरूरी है अब . . . एक बार माँ बनोगी तब ही तुम्हें एक शादीशुदा बीवी की जिम्मेदारियाँ निभानी आएंगी . . . Gynae के यहाँ गयी थी . . .?

SUSANNA. Tests हुए . . . सब normal आया है . . .

RODRIQUES. Then why can't you conceive . . .?

She puts the wooden boot on the floor

SUSANNA. She says कि मुझ में कोई कमी नहीं है . . .

The statement hits the Major like a rock. He is stunned. He raises his amputated leg and starts to caress her with it.

RODRIQUES (*staring into her eyes*). तो अब मैं बिस्तर में भी अपाहिज़ हूँ . . . Hmm . . .?

Suddenly the door opens and Goonga enters, holding a tray with a glass of milk. The Major turns sharply as Goonga watches Susanna crying profusely. He gets up and walks towards Goonga, limping. He bends down on his knees to talk to him.

RODRIQUES. कितनी बार समझाया है, घुसने से पहले knock करना है . . .

He taps hard on his chest with his two fingers.

RODRIQUES. Knock . . . knock.

The little man shakes, so does the tray and the glass of milk on it.

RODRIQUES. अगली बार ऐसे अंदर आया तो यहीं ज़िंदा गाड़ दूंगा तुझे . . . समझा . . .?

He picks the glass and smashes it on the wall. Goonga is startled. He looks back at Susanna who keeps crying helplessly, trying not to make eye contact. Goonga turns and walks away.

Cut to:

Ext. Campfire. Night.

Another drinking session at the campfire. This time Arun, now a young adult, is sitting with the trio.

GHALIB. यही होता है . . . मियाँ . . . जल्दी-जल्दी शादी करो और फिर आराम से पछताओ . . .

Goonga growls something in a low tone.

MAGGIE. Are you mad! . . . दूसरी टांग तोड़ेगा उसकी . . .

MAGGIE. कुछ तरस खा अपने पे, तेरे दोनों अखरोट काट कर कुत्तों को खिला देगा . . . समझा . . .

Goonga makes a lewd gesture towards Maggie and walks away in anger. Arun sees his opportunity and reaches for the beer bottle, but Maggie swats his hand away.

MAGGIE. तेरे दोनों कान उखाड़ के bums पे चिपका दूँगी . . . bastard . . . फिर उल्टा बैठ के पढ़ेगा स्कूल में . . . upside-down . . .

Arun is embarrassed. Maggie looks towards the house where one of the upstairs windows is lit. We see a silhouetted image of Susanna standing at the window, staring into the starry sky.

Cut to:

Ext. Stables. Day.

An illiterate, humble syce walks one of the thoroughbreds out into the sunlight, where the Major is waiting. The horse has been fitted with a saddle and bridle.

The Major turns and snaps his fingers and the frightened groom runs for the stable door, where Goonga is watching.

The dwarf offers them his bucket, and the syce brings it over to the horse and turns it over. The Major uses it to swing himself up into the saddle.

Goonga smiles in anticipation as the Major touches his heels to the horse's flanks. The animal jerks forward and the saddle slips! The Major cries out and lands in the mud with a thud.

Immediately, the syce is there, helping the cursing Major to his feet, but the poor fellow is rewarded with a hail of blows from the Major's riding crop.

Goonga's grin vanishes; he charges forward, yammering in protest. The Major won't let up until the dwarf pulls the riding crop from his hand.

The Major wheels on the little man. Standoff.

RODRIQUES. So. It's a fight you want, is it? दिशुम . . .
दिशुम . . .

Cut to:

Ext. Riding ring. Day.

The syces and a few other servants are perched along the split rail fence, watching a fight that's underway in the centre of the riding ring.

CRACK! CRACK! The hissing, snapping sound of WHIPS rends the air!

The Major and Goonga are both bare-chested, circling each other with long, leather whips. The dwarf's burly torso is covered in wicked lacerations—but the Major is unscathed.

He deftly avoids the little man's flailing lash and takes careful aim at Goonga's eyes. CRACK! The lash flicks out and suddenly, the dwarf drops his whip and topples over, screaming and clawing at his face.

Satisfied, the Major coils up his whip, turns on his heel, and walks away.

Arun comes running towards them as Goonga howls in agony. Blood spills from between the dwarf's fingers; one eye has been plucked out.

A teary-eyed Arun cradles him in his arms as the dwarf howls in pain.

Cut to.

Int. Goonga's hospital room. Day.

The dwarf's face is swathed in bandages; only his one remaining eye is visible. A stony-faced Susanna looks at him while the doctor readies a syringe.

DOCTOR. मुझे पता चला कि यह जन्म से गूंगा और बहरा भी है . . .

SUSANNA. ज़िंदा रह पाएगा . . .?

DOCTOR. Yeah . . . बहादुर है . . . बच जाएगा . . . but we are sorry, हम आँख नहीं बचा सके इसकी . . .

SUSANNA. अब जो देखना है उसके लिए एक आँख काफ़ी है . . . इलाज में कोई कमी ना रहे . . .

Arun sobs in the doorway along with Maggie. Susanna walks past them, her face full of hatred and foreboding.

Cut to:

Ext. Chapel. Night.

The chapel bell tower is an eerie silhouette against the starry sky. The heavy bell is tolling.

Int. Bell tower. Night.

Inside, in the dark, Susanna heaves on the thick rope, rocking the bell back and forth.

  As the sound of the bell continues, Susanna stares in accusation at a carved Jesus nailed to the cross.

Fade out.

Ext. Road. Day.

The open-top Land Rover motors along a dusty country road, stopping alongside Arun who's on his way home from school. Susanna is at the wheel with the Major besides her. Sitting in the back, in charge of several guns, is Ghalib.

  The jeep crosses Arun. Susanna smiles at him while Ghalib playfully pretends to shoot him.

ARUN (*voice-over*). अगली बार मैंने मेजर को आख़िरी बार देखा . . . घने जंगलों में एक man-eating panther की तलाश में जाते हुए . . . सारे शिकारी साथ थे, मगर सबके शिकार भी अलग थे और निशाने भी . . .

Ext. Clearing. Night.

A bleating goat is tied to a big shisham tree at the edge of a forest clearing. Up in the branches, the hunting party has made itself comfortable on a spacious machaan.

Nibbling snacks, the Major cradles a rifle and scans the trees for some sign of movement.

SUSANNA. Can I have a drink tonight . . .?

The Major looks at her with bloodshot eyes. He takes a sip from his whisky glass and pulls her closer and caresses her hair.

MAJOR. No . . .

He starts nuzzling her.

MAJOR. You can't have just one . . . minimum three.

He tries to unbutton her shirt; she stops him.

SUSANNA. We must be very still, very quiet वरना जानवर नहीं आएगा . . .

He brushes her hand away.

MAJOR. मेरे अंदर तो आ गया है . . .

Suddenly, a whisper from Ghalib.

GHALIB. मेजर साब . . . तैनात . . .

Ghalib points to the woods. A pair of shining eyes are moving behind the trees. The Major downs another whisky from his flask, then picks up his rifle and moves to the edge of the platform.

With a firm look in his eyes, Ghalib passes a rifle over to Susanna. Susanna's eyes are cold. The Major kneels at the edge and takes aim.

For a moment, all is still except for the bleating of the goat. Then the panther bounds across the clearing! It leaps right over the goat—up, up to the machaan. Its claws are extended, it's teeth bared.

FREEZE FRAME.

ARUN (*voice-over*). Panther को बकरी में कोई interest नहीं था . . . उसे आदमी की तलाश थी . . .

The Major enters the frame, tumbling down from the machaan. Just before he hits the ground, FREEZE FRAME again.

ARUN (*voice-over*). कहना मुश्किल था कि शराब के नशे में मेजर का पैर फिसला था या फिर किसी ने उसे धक्का दिया, बहरहाल forest guards को दो दिन लगे मेजर को, या मेजर का जो कुछ भी बचा था, उसे ढूँढ़ने में . . .

Cut to.

Int. Chapel. Day.

A rather small funerary urn is on display before the congregation. Alongside it, a colour photograph of the Major.

A choir sings a hymn as the local priest smiles sadly. In nice, clean clothes, Arun stands near the wall, happy to see Susanna in black again.

She's sitting in the front row, her face heavily veiled. Arun's chipper mien fades, however, as he notices that her attention is fixed on a striking young man singing among the tenors.

The camera moves in on Arun. His worried look fills the frame . . .

ARUN (*voice-over*). बहोत कोशिशों के बावजूद मेजर की मौत का रत्ती भर भी दुख नहीं हुआ मुझे . . . किस्मत ने जैसे दूसरा मौका दिया था

मुझे साहेब को पाने का . . . उम्मीद से फूल कर मैं गुब्बारा हुआ जा रहा था . . . पर साहेब को गुब्बारा नहीं guitar चाहिए था . . .

Flashcuts.

At night, the handsome young man sits on top of a grave, strumming his guitar as Susanna notices him from her bedroom window.

As the Major and Susanna drive away from young Arun—heading towards the jungle—we see the same man pass by on a motorcycle. Susanna and the young man make eye contact.

Super—एक दूजे के लिये

Interior. Chapel. Day.

Some months later—same chapel, same guests, same priest. Different music. Now Arun's eyes reflect bitter disappointment.

ARUN (*voice-over*). हिंदुस्तान की लड़कियाँ in general guitar बजाने वाले पर थोड़ा-सा जल्दी मर जाया करती हैं और ये हरामज़ादा तो गाता भी बहुत अच्छा था . . .

Susanna's at the altar, in a white wedding dress. The groom is none other than the handsome chorister. He slips a ring on to her finger . . .

Cut to:

Int. Bedroom. Night.

Susanna and the handsome young groom are naked in the bed sheets, all tangled up in passionate lovemaking.

ARUN (*voice-over*). शादी से पहले इस प्राणी का नाम Jamshed Singh Rathod था . . .

Susanna sits astride her new husband, but as he rolls her on to her back, he pins her arms and whispers in her ear.

JIMMY. आज से मेरा नाम Jimmy है . . . Jimmy Stetson . . . Okay, you call me Jim.

Susanna lays on the bed, lazy in her post-coital lethargy looks at him and whispers.

SUSANNA. And you call me Susie . . .

JIMMY. Susie . . .

SUSANNA. Jim . . .

JIMMY. Susie and Jim.

SUSANNA. Jim and Susie.

BOTH. Made for each other.

They snuggle into each other and start the lovemaking again.
   Pre-lap: guitar chords.

Int. Bedroom. Later.

Munching some grapes, Susanna is propped up against the pillows, listening as her new dream boat, still naked at the foot of the bed, strums a guitar and sings.
   Moved, Susanna holds him tight.

SUSANNA. ये मेरे लिए लिखा है तुमने . . .?

JIMMY (*still playing the guitar*). लिखा नहीं है . . . ये मुझ में से फूटा है . . . My wedding gift to you.

SONG: O *Mama*

Jimmy starts singing again, and the song becomes a lively ballad . . .

Susanna twirls across the room, kicking pillows and vamping it up in the bed sheet. Then she's in Jimmy's arms, covering him in kisses. She's happy.

Dissolve to:

Int. Bombay recording studio. Day.

Jimmy's at the microphone, singing another verse of the same song. He's focused solely on Susanna, who's seated with a producer on the other side of the glass.

Now the lyrics are sexy enough to make her blush, laugh, and cover her face.

A few studio employees drift in to listen; they like what they're hearing.

Dissolve to:

Int. Stables. Night.

Goonga and all the scyes are gathered around an old television, on which Jimmy's song is being played. It has become a huge hit.

One of the grooms grabs Goonga, and makes him dance. The dwarf's face is covered in scar tissue, and he wears an eye patch.

Then, sudden change in the soundtrack—the old TV show Krishi Darshan. *Everything stops, and they see that a visibly jealous Arun has changed the channel.*

A syce turns the channel back to the song and the dancing resumes. Maggie enters the stable only to find herself in Goonga's arms, spinning past the thoroughbreds.

As the song moves into its final chorus, the arrangement and vocalist undergo an awful change, becoming a mockery of the successful single.

Dissolve to:

Int. Recording studio. Day.

The producer, grim-faced, sits in the recording studio alongside Susanna, who's aghast.

Standing before them, singing and playing a harmonium, is Benjamin Chaterjee aka Chatty, a portly performer with long hair, who is working his way through the very same song.

As he finishes, the producer fixes him with an icy stare.

MANAGER. सबूत क्या है कि ये गाना तुम्हारा है . . .?

CHATTY. College में compose किया था मैंने ये गाना . . . Jamshed मेरे band में backing vocals गाया करता था . . . चोर निकला . . . Where the hell is he?

He whips out a cassette and hands it over to the manager

CHATTY. और सबूत भी है . . . दो साल पहले T-Series ने निकाला था . . .

The manager looks at his subordinate.

MANAGER. Which series is that—T?

The subordinate shrugs his shoulders.

MANAGER. अब क्या चाहिए तुम्हें . . .?

CHATTY. इज्ज़त . . .

The manager looks at Susanna, who is appalled.

MANAGER दे दें . . .?

Cut to:

Int. Recording studio. Later.

With the dyspeptic producer looking on, Susanna sits at his desk, writing a cheque.
    As she hands it over, Chatty grins and picks out an arpeggio on his harmonium.

CHATTY. Thanks, man . . . एक और number है मेरे पास, खरीदेंगी ? Hit है एकदम . . . Superhit . . .

He launches into a slow tortured Love Ballad.
    Pre-lap: Chorus.

Cut to:

Int. Concert hall. Night.

SONG: दिल दिल है

An excited Delhi audience, mostly female, is yelling and applauding. A banner hangs from the balcony: 'We Love You Jimmy!'
    And Jimmy's front and centre on stage. His sequined shirt and jeans are glittering in the spotlight. Behind him, a six-piece backup band.

JIMMY. ये गाना आज तक कभी किसी और ने नहीं सुना है . . . ये सिर्फ उसके लिए है और उसके लिए रहेगा . . . जो आज हमारे बीच मौजूद है . . . मेरी हमसफ़र, मेरी साँस . . . मेरी धड़कन . . . मेरी जान, Susie!

He points towards a corner, where Susanna sits. As the audience gets to its feet, the camera slowly moves to her. Susanna tries to smile.

ARUN (*voice-over*). Jimmy के झूठ से अनजान बने रहने के लिए साहेब ने खुद से सच कहना बंद कर दिया था . . . मगर झूठ तो शुरूआत थी . . . Jimmy के rainbow में बाक़ी रंग तो उभरने अभी बाक़ी थे . . .

Int. Recording studio. Day.

A dozen musicians sip tea and smoke as the worried manager paces back and forth, looking at his watch.
The film producer arrives chewing paan, as a person holds a vessel for him to spit into.
The producer looks at the manager with piercing eyes.

MANAGER. कब के निकल चुके हैं घर से . . . अब तो फ़िक्र होने लगी है मुझे . . .

The producer spits the paan and wipes his lips.

PRODUCER. शब्बीर कुमार की भी हिम्मत नहीं है ऐसा करने की . . . समझा . . . यह बप्पी दा का गान है . . .

PRODUCER. और बप्पी दा के गान में कितना violin बजता है पता है . . .? 100 violin . . . पैसा कौन भरेगा साला . . . तेरा बाप . . .

Cut to:

Int. Susanna's Panchgani house. Day.

Susanna in her Panchgani house writes a cheque and hands it over to the manager, who smiles sheepishly.

ARUN (*voice-over*). ये नशा सिर्फ शोहरत का नशा होता तो उतर भी जाता मगर Jimmy के सर पे और कई नशे सवार थे . . .

Int. Disco/Hotel room. Night.

Jimmy at a table with some girls wearing revealing outfits, and an ingratiating drug peddler. They are examining some white powder in a clear envelope. The peddler starts to heat the powder over a candle in a spoon.

PEDDLER. हो कहाँ Sir ji आप, वहाँ Berlin की दीवार गिर चुकी, V.P. Singh की सरकार गिर चुकी, और आप अभी तक cocaine पे अटके हो, इसे कहते हैं . . . Heroin!

The peddler fills the injection with an liquid from the spoon.
He ties a rubber string on Jimmy's arm and administers the
injection into his vein.

Cut to:

Ext. Concert hall. Night.

The poster next to the box office reads: 'TONIGHT: JIMMY
STETSON'.
   From inside, the dull thud of people stamping their feet!

ANNOUNCER (*voice-over*). देवियो और सज्जनो . . . बस थोड़ा
सा इंतज़ार और . . . फिर संगीत की दुनिया का जादूगर, आप और ये
रात . . .

Angry boos and cat calls. Angry ticket-holders are streaming
from the theatre. Someone rips down the poster.
   Policemen escort the cowering manager through the mob
as he ducks a hail of tossed shoes and fruit.

Cut to:

Int. Susanna's house. Day.

A grumpy Goonga removes a large stash of Rs 100 currency
notes from a bag and places it on the table as the manager
sits opposite with a broken, plastered hand and a few band-
aids on his face. Susanna looks on in disappointment.

Cut to:

Ext./Int. The Taj Hotel—Bombay. Night.

The Taj Hotel at the Gateway of India. A doorbell rings a
few times on the soundtrack. Susanna waits for the door to
be opened. After a moment, a tall, half-naked Tibetan girl
answers the door. She is breathless and giggling.

TIBETAN GIRL. What is it . . .?

SUSANNA. Jimmy . . .

The girl looks back, giggling.

TIBETAN GIRL. Jim, you have a fan here.

Jimmy, only in his underwear, enters the room chasing another half-naked North-eastern girl, and pins her down on the sofa.

JIMMY. धप्पा . . .

NORTH-EASTERN GIRL. Cheating . . . it's cheating. Jimmy is a cheater!

The Tibetan girl also runs back to the two of them on the couch.

TIBETAN GIRL. Jimmy is a cheater . . .

A playful fight ensues between the three of them. Susanna walks inside—the room is littered with used dishes and liquor bottles. Suddenly Jimmy notices Susanna standing near the piano which is laden with overflowing ashtrays, he is now sandwiched between the two girls. His smile vanishes. He slowly forces himself free of the girls and walks towards her.

JIMMY. Susie . . . कब आयीं तुम . . .? Inform क्यूँ नहीं किया मुझे . . .? पहले . . .!

Both the girls follow Jimmy and stand each at his shoulder. He looks at Susanna looking at them.

JIMMY. Don't misunderstand, Susie . . . We are just friends.

TIBETAN GIRL. Just . . .

NORTH-EASTERN GIRL. . . . friends.

They giggle and Jimmy also smiles, but suddenly gathers himself and speaks seriously.

JIMMY. हम लोग पता है क्या कर रहे थे . . .?

He looks at both the girls, who giggle.

JIMMY. खेल रहे थे . . .

TIBETAN GIRL. I-Spy.

NORTH-EASTERN GIRL. Hide and seek.

JIMMY. तुम भी खेलोगी . . .?

Susanna is disgusted. Suddenly the Tibetan girl screams and smacks his arm.

TIBETAN GIRL. Jimmy चोर . . .?

The girls disappear into the bedroom; Jimmy runs after them.

Int. Hotel bedroom. Continuous.

All three race around, firing their ray guns. Susanna follows and discovers a hypodermic needle and packets of heroin on the bedside table.
    Jimmy comes up behind her.

JIMMY. Susie . . . you will have to try this for me . . . It's spiritual . . .

He injects himself and takes a deep breath. The girls start to prepare their doses. Jimmy walks to Susanna.

JIMMY. इसके बाद मेरी creativity सौगुना बढ़ जाती है . . .

Blinking, he comes close to her and pecks her on her cheek.

JIMMY. जानती हो मैंने कितने नए songs बनाए हैं . . .

Woozy, he leans back.

JIMMY. . . . तुम्हारे लिए . . .? Guess . . .!

Firing her toy gun, the shrieking Tibetan girl runs past, knocking him over. CRASH! He falls on to one of the guitars.

JIMMY. Jimmy's dead! Jimmy's dead!

Cut to:

Ext. Susanna's house. Day.

Susanna leads a shaky Jimmy from a taxi into her grand house in Panchgani. He's got a bandage on the back of his head. Ghalib, Maggie and Goonga are at the front door, watching impassively.

ARUN (*voice-over*). इस बार साहेब को ज़िद थी . . . रिश्ता बचाने की ज़िद . . . किसी भी क़ीमत पर वो हारने को तैयार नहीं थी . . . मिज़ाज से साहेब romantic थी . . . A die-hard hopeless romantic. इसीलिए तो सारी उम्र सच्चे प्यार की तलाश में भटकती रही . . . बहुत सालों बाद एक बार बड़ी heavy urdu में कहते सुना था . . . कि मियाँ Arun . . . इश्क़ रेगिस्तानों का सराब है . . . a mirage . . . उसका एहसास तो होता है . . . पर वो होता नहीं . . .

Int. Bedroom. Day.

Jimmy is tied to the bed post. He strains against the ropes, pleading and bleating like a goat being taken to the slaughter.

JIMMY. Susie . . . I am your Jim . . . क्यूँ कर रही हो तुम मेरे साथ ऐसा . . . मैं drugs को हाथ भी नहीं लगाऊंगा . . . तुम्हारी कसम . . . Susie please खोल दो मुझे . . .

Susanna calmly steps aside to allow a local doctor to approach with a loaded hypodermic needle. Jimmy's tone changes.

JIMMY. You bitch . . . एक बार खुला तो गला घोट दूंगा तेरा . . . Jamshed Singh Rathod नाम है मेरा . . . राजपूत हूँ . . . तेरे टुकड़े करके कुत्तों को खिला दूँगा मैं . . .

The doctor looks at Susanna. She nods at Maggie, who walks like a giant and holds Jimmy's shoulders. Ghalib and Goonga clutch each of his feet. The doctor administers the injection; Jimmy grunts and starts to cool down. The doctor takes Susanna aside.

DOCTOR. I can recommend a good rehab facility in Pune—a very private, excellent one.

SUSANNA. No, Doctor. Thanks . . . अब उसे अकेले नहीं छोड़ सकती मैं . . . उसमें जान बंद है मेरी . . .

Ext. Garden. Day.

Jimmy, clean-shaven and well-rested, moves through the flower beds with a watering can. It's a nice day; the birds are chirping.

ARUN (*voice-over*). और फिर साहेब की जान बेहतर हो चली . . . Jimmy अब सुधरने लगा था . . . मगर फिर भी वो एक बाज़ की तरह उसे अपने निगाहों के पहरे में रखती थीं . . . हर दम . . . उन्हें अंदाजा

नहीं था कि drug addicts एक बार पकड़े जाने के बाद बहोत चालाक, ज्यादा ख़बरदार और होशियार हो जाते हैं . . . champion धोखेबाज़ . . .

Int. Salon. Day.

Sergeant Keemat Lal, 40, a local cop in neatly pressed khakis, roams around the library, admiring Susanna's father's gun collection. He's carrying a long package.

He pauses before a photograph of a very young Susanna and her father standing under a palm tree at an elegant hotel in Goa.

The man turns to see Susanna entering. He's a bit overawed in the presence of her ladyship.

KEEMAT. मादाम . . .

His eyes return to a shotgun on display.

KEEMAT. कल एक drug peddler के पास बरामद हुई है ये . . .

He displays the gun in his hands.

KEEMAT. देखते ही पहचान गया था . . . इतनी हसीन और ख़ूबसूरत चीज़ का हक़दार और कोई हो ही नहीं सकता है . . .

Susanna looks at him sharply. Keemat fumbles.

KEEMAT. बेशक़ीमती भी है . . . क्या क़ीमत होगी इसकी मादाम . . .?

Susanna inspects the gun.

SUSANNA. बेशक़ीमती चीजों की क़ीमत नहीं हुआ करती है inspector . . . आपका नाम . . .?

KEEMAT. क़ीमत . . .

Susanna looks at him again; this time he smiles.

KEEMAT. इंस्पेक्टर क़ीमत लाल . . .

Susanna smiles back.

SUSANNA. Muzzle loader NX 6 . . . Amongst the first guns to be brought to India by the soldiers of the British Raj . . . मेरे father की favourite gun हुआ करती थी . . .

KEEMAT. आपके सब नौकरों से मिलना चाहूंगा मैं . . .

Susanna looks out the window. She can see Jimmy, sprawled under a tree, puffing a cigarette and strumming his guitar. He is serenading his dog.

KEEMAT. किसी ख़ास पर शक़-शुबहा है आपको . . .?

She turns to face him; he smiles.

KEEMAT. मादाम . . .

SUSANNA. यहाँ के नौकर, मालिकों से ज्यादा वफ़ादार हैं . . .

KEEMAT (*nodding*). मादाम . . .

SUSANNA. आप चाहें तो मुझे मेरे नाम से बुला सकते हैं . . .

She offers her hand to shake.

SUSANNA. Susanna . . .

Keemat's eyes pop out. He takes her hand and blushes.

KEEMAT. ऐसा कैसे . . . मादाम . . . जी . . . शुक्रिया . . . फिर भी . . . नहीं वैसे . . . फिर कभी . . . कोशिश . . . ख़ैर होगा नहीं . . . अभी तो . . . अजीब है . . . पर अब . . . छोड़िए . . .

He keeps blushing and shaking her hand, making no sense at all.

Cut to:

Int. Shower. Day.

A light rain falls outside the bathroom window.

Half-hidden in billowing clouds of steam, Jimmy's in the shower, wrapping plastic tubing around his forearm and readying his hypodermic needle.

Int. Bedroom. Same.

Meanwhile, Susanna goes through the pockets of Jimmy's jeans. She finds a bag of heroin.

Emptying out the closet, she discovers a couple more bags of white powder in his cowboy boots.

She heaves off the mattress and spots a plastic bag of dope resting on the box spring.

Then she's pulling out and turning over desk drawers. Sure enough, more drugs.

Inside the bathroom, the sound of the shower suddenly stops.

Int. Bathroom. Same.

Jimmy, glassy-eyed and high, puts on a terrycloth robe and tucks his hypodermic needle behind a loosened tile on the wall.

He looks in the mirror, combs his hair, and frowns, hearing a noise outside the door.

Int. Bedroom. Continuous.

Jimmy emerges from the bathroom and looks around the bedroom. Everything is neat as a pin. And no one is there.

The camera moves in on Jimmy's face.

Pre-lap: the tolling bell—in the rain.

Cut to:

Int. Kitchen. Night.

Maggie stands in the kitchen in her bathrobe. She's listening to the sound of the bell.

Wearing pyjamas, Ghalib enters, reacting to the ominous sound. He and Maggie exchange a look.

Ext. Stables. Same.

Goonga comes outside wearing oversized gum-boots and carrying an umbrella in his hand. He looks over towards the chapel, where the bell is ringing.

He can see the silhouetted steeple in the moonlight—but no lights are on.

Int. Bell tower. Night.

Susanna, dressed in black, is pulling on the bell rope for all she's worth. CLANG! CLANG!

Dissolve to:

Ext. Garden. Day.

The rain has stopped but puddles of water are all over the place. Arun comes racing past the stables.

He runs on—up the drive, and past the cemetery. He exits the frame, while the camera lingers on a figure in the background leaning against a headstone.

Arun walks back into the frame, recognizing Jimmy.

Arun walks closer with mounting dread.

From his POV, we come closer to Jimmy, whose head hangs low, dripping rainwater. Jimmy's dog is there, too, shivering and whimpering.

On the ground, a hypodermic needle and bent spoon. Arun touches Jimmy's shoulder—and Jimmy topples over, cold and dead.

Cut to:

Ext. Cemetery. Later.

In the driveway, cops load a stretcher bearing Jimmy's corpse into a waiting hearse.
Standing at the tombstone is Keemat Lal. A flunky is holding an umbrella over his head.
Arun is watching from a respectful distance.
A trail of bent grass and crushed flowers lead to the tombstone.
The inspector wanders through the tombstones, checking the ground.

KEEMAT (*to the flunky*). ऐ छाता बंद कर!

Ext. Naag Temple well. Day.

Now Keemat is at the edge of the well, staring down into its shadowy depths.

ARUN. संभाल के सर . . . बड़े ज़हरीले साँप है यहाँ . . . नाग देवता के मंदिर में . . .

KEEMAT. नाग देवता का मंदिर?

Keemat starts to walk towards the tree .

KEEMAT. मगर मादाम तो क्रिस्तानी है . . .

ARUN. Father Christian थे साहेब के, पर माँ हिंदू . . . थीं . . . उन्होंने बनवाया था ये मंदिर . . . साहेब रोज़ सुबह दूध चढ़ाती हैं नाग देवता को . . .

KEEMAT. कैसे . . .?

ARUN. नीचे जा कर . . .

KEEMAT. साँपों से डर नहीं लगता उन्हें . . .?

ARUN. नहीं वो पालतू हैं उनके . . . और उनके नज़रिये से इंसान साँप से ज्यादा ज़हरीले और खतरनाक होते हैं.

Keemat is amused.

KEEMAT. वाह वाह . . . वाह वाह . . .

Suddenly a snake crosses over Keemat Lal's foot on the grass.

ARUN. Sir साँप . . .

Keemat freaks out and falters back. He takes stumbles a few steps behind and falls to the ground. Arun runs up to him.

ARUN. Sir आप ठीक हैं ना . . .?

Keemat is regaining his breath. He nods. All of a sudden something catches his eye, he looks down to see footprints in the moist earth. His expression changes, as he points at one footprint in particular.

KEEMAT. किसका पंजा है ये . . .?

Arun looks down.

ARUN. किसी का भी हो सकता है Sir . . .

Keemat starts to follow the footprints.

KEEMAT. किसी का भी नहीं, ये क़ातिल का पंजा है . . .

Arun trails Keemat to the back door of the house.

ARUN. क़ातिल . . .?

Keemat suddenly grabs a bewildered Arun from under his arms and drags him across the ground as if he were a dead body, retracing the 'killer's' steps.

KEEMAT (*theorizing*). हाँ क़ातिल . . . हो सकता है ये ख़ुदकुशी दिखावा हो और असल में यह वारदात कल्ल की है . . .

He inspects the footprints more closely,

KEEMAT. एक पैर में 6 उंगली किसके हैं यहाँ . . .?

Arun shrugs his shoulders.

ARUN. पता नही . . .

KEEMAT. जूते खोल अपने . . .

ARUN. जी . . .?

Keemat shrieks.

KEEMAT. जूते खोल !

Arun hurriedly opens his shoes, and Keemat looks at his feet.

Cut to:

Ext. Stables. Day.

Close shot of many bare feet.
    The servants and workers stand in line as Keemat Lal inspects the toes of each and everyone. Arun and Ghalib follow, their feet bare.

KEEMAT. कोई बचा तो नहीं है . . .?

GHALIB. नहीं . . .

Arun wants to say something but Ghalib covers his mouth.

ARUN. एक है . . .

Keemat sharply turns to Arun.

KEEMAT. कौन . . .?

A voice comes from behind.

SUSANNA. मैं . . .

Susanna is standing there in a floppy sun hat, sheer blouse and mini-skirt. Keemat's eyes go down from her breasts all the way to her bare feet. Maggie strolls up with an umbrella, wearing sneakers. Keemat is too dazzled by Susanna to notice.
   Keemat retrieves Susanna's sandals and sits next to her feet.

KEEMAT. क्यों शर्मिंदा करती हैं . . . ख़ामख़ाह में पैरों को मैला कर डाला . . . आप भी मादाम . . .

Susanna cuts him short.

SUSANNA. मादाम नहीं—Susanna . . .

Keemat blushes as usual. He helps her put on the sandals, mumbling in utter pleasure and disbelief.

KEEMAT. आप भी . . . बस . . . ऐवें . . . मैं कहाँ . . . आप तो . . . ख़ैर . . . मज़ाक . . . ठीक ही है . . . पर ग़लत . . . मैं क्या कहूँ . . .? आगे से सही . . . आपकी मर्ज़ी . . . वैसे अच्छा ही है . . . आप पर बुरा . . . नहीं . . . छोड़िए . . . फिर कभी . . . कैसे होगा . . .

He blathers on. Susanna smiles.
Fade to black.

ARUN (*voice-over*). सुना है Jesus ने अपने आख़री दिन वादी-ए-कश्मीर में गुज़ारे थे । साहेब उनकी तलाश में कश्मीर गयीं तो, पर वहां उन्हें Jesus नहीं मौहम्मद मिल गये। मौहम्मद वसीउल्लाह ख़ान उर्फ़ मुसाफ़िर।

Super—मुसाफ़िर हूँ यारों

Int. House. Night.

Angry shouts and cries of hundreds of men roaring out loud in anger, calling out 'जय श्री राम, जय श्री राम' resonate on the soundtrack.

On a television set we see the disturbing images of the Babri Masjid demolition.

In silhouette we see the face of a man watching the broadcast—angry, hurt, enraged.

Ext. Shalimar Garden. Dusk.

In the twilight, the snow-capped Kashmiri mountain peaks are glowing pink. It is a stunning sight.

A soulful, melodious voice recites a poem decrying the 1992 demolition of the Babri Masjid.

WASIULLAH.

रोज़ उठते धूएं की कालिख से
उस तरफ आसमां का इक टुकड़ा
सारा दिन अब सियाह रहता है
उस के नीचे न कोई सजदा करे
सर झुका के जर्मीं पे रखने से
अब खुदा पॉव खींच लेता है
कूड़े करकट की ढेरियों में अभी
ठंढी लाशों के सर सुलगते हैं
टांगों बाँहों की हड्डियों के लिए
लड़ते रहते हैं भूखे चौपाये
जिसने भी पहले दाँत मारे हैं

हड्डी बोटी का हक़ उसी का है
मज़हब वाले पूछते हैं अब
किसने पहले कुदाल मारी थी ?
कोई कहता है एक मस्जिद थी
कोई कहता है एक मंदिर था
सर झुका के ज़मीं पे रखने से
अब ख़ुदा पाँव खींच लेता है
उसको भी अब यक़ीं नहीं आता
इस ज़मीं पर उसी का इक घर था।

Ext./Int. Lawn or Building. Continuous.

On stage the poet Wasiullah Khan, 40, reaches the final verse of his poem. He is refined and dreamily dressed in a black achkan and white kurta, with a typical woollen Kashmiri cap on his head. As the audience stands and applauds, the camera moves in to the centre of the front row, where a woman—clad from head to toe in a flowing black burqa—looks at the poet.

It's Susanna. In the audience Ghalib, Goonga and Maggie are also present.

ARUN (*voice-over*). साहेब का इश्क़ बदला और इस बार इश्क़ के साथ नाम और मज़हब भी बदल गया। Susanna Anna-Marie Johannes अब सुल्ताना वसीउल्लाह ख़ान थीं . . .

Int. Kashmir house. Day.

Susanna offers her prayers.

ARUN (*voice-over*). वो अब पाँच वक़्त की नमाज़ी थीं . . .

Int. Painting exhibition. Day.

SONG: बेक़राँ

Susanna strolls past paintings at an exhibition in Delhi. She hears a beautiful voice resonating the following words:

WASIULLAH.
> बेक़राँ हैं बेक़राँ, आँखें बंद कीजे ना,
> डूबने लगे हैं हम साँस लेने दीजे ना

She follows it to an adjoining book shop. We now see the source of the soothing words—Wasiullah, standing atop a stage, reciting his poem. Wearing spectacles, he is reading from his book.

WASIULLAH.
> ग़ैर लड़की से कहे कोई
> मुनासिब तो नहीं
> एक शायर को, मगर इतना सा हक़ और भी है
> पास जाए और अदब से कह दे
> इक ज़रा चेहरा उधर कीजे, इनायत होगी
> आपको देख के बड़ी देरी से मेरी साँस रूकी है

Int. Book shop. Continuous.

It's a public reading of new poems by the poet Wasiullah Khan, from his book Musafir.

ARUN (*voice-over*). वसीउल्लाह से अपनी मुलाक़ात को उन्होंने अल्लाह मियाँ की मर्ज़ी क़रार दिया . . . वर्ना उर्दू, ग़ज़ल और मुशायरों से उनका दूर–दूर तक वास्ता नहीं था . . .

Ext. Susanna's Panchgani house. Day.

Susanna sits motionless on a swing in her garden as the wind blows the dry leaves across the lawn.

ARUN (*voice-over*). Jimmy के बाद उदास पतझड़ के कई मौसमों से गुज़री थीं साहेब . . .

Int. Puraana Qila. Day.

Wasiullah recites another poem in some other Mushaira. Susanna sits in the crowd as a sudden rain shower sweeps in.

ARUN (*voice-over*). फिर एक दिन वसीउल्लाह और उसकी शायरी उन पर ऐसी टूट कर बरसी कि उसके बाद भीगी–भीगी–सी रहने लगीं . . .

Int. Backstage. Same.

A completely drenched Susanna approaches Wasiullah Khan for an autograph. Wasiullah stops signing and looks at her walking through the crowd. He walks to her; she offers her palm.

Wasiullah drops his pen away and writes his name in Urdu over her palm. The heavenly shower of rain comes again and starts to drench both of them The romantic poem continues on the soundtrack.

Ext. Kashmir roads. Day.

Susanna and Waisullah Khan walk in silence among the beautiful, serene landscape of Kashmir. Wasiullah holds his pet, a small white kitten in his arm and caresses her softly.

ARUN (*voice-over*). फिर वो अपने दिल और घर के साथ कश्मीर में जा बसीं . . .

Saans—montage.

Very much in love, Susanna and Wasiullah sit together as they watch a senior poet recite a couplet at a Mushaira in Triveni, Delhi.

The smitten couple attend another Mushaira at the Habitat Centre in Delhi. Wasiuallah dedicates one of his couplets to her.

Wasiullah conducts a lecture in a classroom at Kashmir University. Susanna stands outside the classroom, teasing him, trying to distract him, to grab his attention. She has brought him his lunch.

After the lecture they hurriedly get into his car which is parked in front of the University building. The chivalrous Wasiullah opens the passenger door for Susanna and shuts it after she is seated. They drive away.

The two of them on a shikara, paddling their way through the chilly waters of Dal Lake, taking in the crisp evening air.

As the couple pass an army bunker, a tense Susanna looks over at the grim soldiers. Wasiullah lovingly holds her hand as they walk passed the barbed wire fencing of the bunker.

Susanna and Wasiullah in separate sections of the Jamia Mosque in Srinagar, offering namaz.

In their house, Susanna stands alone on a pedestal, dressed like Wasiullah, doing her best to seriously recite a couplet as her husband sits on the floor in front of her and laughs his heart out at her attempt.

Ext. Puraana Qila. Day.

A poster advertising another poetry recital by the poet is plastered on a billboard.

SONG: आवारा

WASIULLAH.
आवारा आवारा
हवा पे रख्खे सूखे पत्ते
आवारा
पाँव ज़मी पर रखते ही उड़ लेते हैं दोबारा
ना शाख़ जुड़े ना जड़ पकड़े
मौसम मौसम बंजारा

The poet now suddenly seems a little older than before. We notice grey hair on his stubble and tousled mane. He looks tired and unhappy. Susanna, who now has awkwardly timid body language, is wearing large sunglasses at this point.

The couple step in front of the poster as several students cluster around them, taking photos. The poet modestly signs someone's autograph book. As Susanna quietly watches this, we notice she has a small scratch on her face and a cut on her lower lip.

A new voice-over poem begins, in which the poet describes his lonely quest for transcendence.

Ext. Puraana Qila. Day.

Susanna is standing amidst the magnificent structure alone, as the setting sun shimmers in the background. A sudden gust of wind blows dust and dry leaves on to her.

She covers herself in a shawl as she continues to stand in solitude, watching the setting sun, confronting the dust-storm head on!

The storm gets worse as even larger clouds of dust and hundreds of dry leaves almost assault her. She still stands there, majestic and statuesque against the twilight.

Ext. Taj Mahal. Day.

Visiting the Taj Mahal, Susanna and the poet pose for a photograph. Susanna playfully refuses to take off her sunglasses, so the amused poet dons a pair of his own.

Ext. School in Kashmir. Day.

Paying a visit to a primary school, the poet and Susanna admire some student art. When one of the kids gives Susanna a hug, she winces.

Int. Wasiullah's Kashmir house—bedroom. Day.

Susanna is at her make-up table, daubing cosmetics on to her cheek with great care. Finally, satisfied, she puts on her big sunglasses, ready to face the world.

Int/Ext. Road to Gulmarg. Day.

Travelling shots—Susanna and Wasiullah travel in silence

along the scenic roads of Kashmir. She is wearing her large
sunglasses as she quietly stares out of the window.

Int. Wasiullah's house—top floor. Day.

The poet is reciting his poem for a hundred invited guests.
Maggie, Ghalib and Goonga are attending to the guests.
But visibly there is something else on their minds. Their Miss
Saheb is not a part of the gathering.
The poet reaches his last poetic stanza:

WASIULLAH.
चल मैं तेरे साथ ही चलता हूँ ऐ यार फक़ीरी में
सुख मिलता है भजन वचन और तेरी कहत कबीरी में . . .

Int. Wasiullah's house—bedroom. Continuous.

As we hear the poetic stanza in the soundtrack, we see a
sorrowful Susanna, sitting alone in her bedroom, staring out
of the window.

ARUN (*voice-over*). और फिर एक दिन सच में वसीउल्लाह अपनी तलाश
के सफ़र पर निकल पड़े . . . कभी वापस ना आने के लिए . . .

Fade to black.

Ext. Arun's college canteen. Day.

In the bustling food court, a few college students read the
headline of a local newspaper carrying a glamorous photograph
of Susanna:
    THE MERRY WIDOW OF PANCHGANI
    Third Husband Vanishes from Kashmir!
    Literary World Fears Worst!

STUDENT 1. वसीउल्लाह मुसाफ़िर का आख़िरी शेर . . . इरशाद
है . . .
'दूर हो जाएंगे सूरज की तरह . . .
हम ना कहते थे उछालो हमको'

Laughter from the other students. Arun, now 25, enters the canteen and sits down. One of the other boys nudges Student 1.

STUDENT 2. सुराग़ बताने वाले को 1 लाख रूपये का ईनाम बेगम सुल्ताना की तरफ से . . . ना नौ मन तेल होगा ना सुल्ताना नाचेगी . . .

The students have a hearty laugh as one turns to Arun and asks:

STUDENT 3. Arun . . . कुछ clue दे यार . . . एक लाख रूपए का सवाल है . . .

Arun smiles, gets up and walks over.

STUDENT 3. 50:50 . . . Fair deal . . . What say . . .?

He winks at Arun amid mischievous snickering.

ARUN Yeah . . . very fair . . .

He bends down, close to the student's ear.

ARUN. Clue दूँ . . . सच में . . .?

The student nods. Arun starts to whisper something, then suddenly bites down! The student screams in pain, but Arun has his bleeding ear clenched in his teeth! Student 2 kicks Arun in the stomach, forcing Arun to release his victim. It's a violent fight with chairs and rods. Arun lashes out in a blind rage.

Jump cut to:

Int. Jail cell. Day.

Arun, in torn clothes and bruised all over, squats behind bars in a police station. Keemat Lal is sitting outside the cell with his leg over a table. He reads a poem from Wasiullah Khan's latest book.

KEEMAT.
सब्र हर बार इख़्तियार किया,
हमसे होता नहीं हज़ार किया . . . वाह . . .

He looks at the book cover, an arty, gauzy photo of Susanna.

KEEMAT. किस किस के कान काटोगे शहर में . . . यहाँ के सबसे बड़े वकील का बेटा है वो . . .

A constable comes running.

CONSTABLE. Sir! Sir! . . . बाहर चलिए . . .

KEEMAT. क्यों . . . तेरी अम्मा आयी है बाहर . . .

CONSTABLE. नहीं, आपकी . . .

KEEMAT. हैं . . .?

CONSTABLE. मादाम . . .

Keemat takes a moment to absorb the information. He starts smiling and stammering, riveted anew by Susanna's photograph.

KEEMAT. ये भी . . . पता नहीं . . . ख़ैर . . . चलो . . .

He looks at the photograph .
Cut to:

Ext. Road outside the police station. Day.

A stony-faced Susanna sits in her car, wearing her big black sunglasses. Goonga is at the wheel while Maggie and Ghalib stand nearby.

Keemat still holds Wasiullah's book.

KEEMAT (*to Susanna*). आपने क्यों तक़लीफ़ की भला . . . मुझे बुलवा लिया होता . . .

The constable brings the official register from inside followed by the disheveled Arun. Keemat shifts the poetry book under his arm and passes the register to Susanna through the car window.

KEEMAT. यहाँ . . . यहाँ पे दस्तख़त . . . बस . . .

He takes back the register and hands it to the constable.

KEEMAT. बहोत अफ़सोस हुआ मुसाफ़िर साहब का सुनकर . . . मगर मुझे उम्मीद है कि वो वापस आएंगे . . .

He steps close to her.

KEEMAT. और उम्मीद पर तो दुनिया क़ायम है . . .

Susanna won't look at him. He fumbles and the poetry book drops from his armpit, landing at Maggie's feet. Arun bends down to retrieve it, but freezes: Maggie's got six toes! Arun instinctively looks at Keemat, who hasn't noticed.
    Kneeling, Keemat lovingly looks at Susanna's photograph on the book. He brushes off the dirt, picks it up and stands alongside Arun.

KEEMAT (*to Arun*). अब आगे से college पढ़ने जाना बरख़ुरदार, लड़ने नहीं.

Susanna softly whispers.

SUSANNA. College से नाम कट चुका है . . . और शायद ये इंसानों नहीं, जानवरों के साथ रहने के लायक़ ही हैं . . .

Arun looks down. The camera closes in on Maggie's six toes.

Cut to:

Ext. Campfire. Night.

The drinking session. Goonga and Maggie are roasting fresh corn over the fire. Ghalib offers a beer to Arun, who doesn't take the can but keeps looking into the flames, lost in deep thought.

GHALIB अरे पी ले यारा . . . साहेब का गुस्सा पारे की तरह है, यूँ चढ़ा और यूँ उतरा . . . थोड़े दिन रूक, फिर नाम जुड़ जाएगा college में . . . उनपे जो गुज़री है ना कश्मीर में, अंदाज़ा नहीं है तुझे . . .

Ghalib opens a can and Arun takes a sip from it.

ARUN. क्या हुआ . . .?

MAGGIE (*gulping down her drink*). कुछ होता ही तो नहीं था . . .

All three burst into a laughter. Arun is curious.

ARUN. क्या . . . क्या नहीं होता था . . .

Goonga grunts something, while lying on the ground, and they burst into more vigorous laughter this time.

ARUN. क्या हुआ . . .?

GHALIB. तूने पूछा क्या नही होता था . . . ? गूंगा बोला वही जो तूने अभी तक किया नही हैं . . .

ARUN. क्या . . .?

GHALIB. Ping Pong.

MAGGIE. Ding Dong.

GHALIB. Pom Pom.

MAGGIE. Tring tring.

They roll down on the ground laughing. Arun also smiles.
Cut to:

Int. Wasiullah's house—bedroom. Night.

Flashback. Wasiullah trying his best to be tender to Susanna
in bed. But he finally fails to arouse himself and slaps Susanna
hard.
   Susanna is shocked as he slaps her again and again.
Susanna cries, Wasiullah looks down at himself—a sadistic
smile appears on his lips.
Cut to:

Int. Wasiullah's house—bedroom. Night.

Later, he calmly strokes Susanna, who is black and blue. She
cries silently, looking at the cat sleeping on the carpet.

GHALIB (*voice-over*). वसीउल्लाह ख़ान दो रास्तों का मुसाफ़िर
था . . . एक रास्ता दिन का जिस पे वो बहोत ही नेक दिल, नर्म, जैसे
बकरी का मेमना, और दूसरा रात का, जहाँ एक हैवान उसके अंदर घुस जाता
था . . . अपनी औरत को जब तलक जी भर के मार ना ले, उसमें कुछ
जागता नहीं था . . .

Int. Wasiullah's house—bedroom. Day.

Susanna in front of the mirror, looking at her bruised face.
She picks up a make-up brush and starts to apply a base.

GHALIB (*voice-over*). शुरू शुरू में, Miss साहेब make-up से अपनी
चोटें छुपा लेती थीं मगर जब मार–पीट का यह सिलसिला बरक़रार रहा तो वो
दूसरे कमरे में सोने लगीं . . . अलहदा.
Cut to:

Int. Wasiullah's house—bedroom. Night.

The poet stands at Susanna's bedroom door. He holds a bouquet of roses in one hand and his cat in the other. He's about to knock when he stops, his face full of guilt and indecision.

Inside, Susanna is reading Anna Karenina. *Wasiullah decides not to knock, but as he turns away, his cat meows.*

Susanna's eyes shift from her book to the door. Outside, Wasiullah shuts his eyes in irritation. Susanna opens the door to find him there, trying to smile. He hands her the flowers, then walks away. After a few steps, he returns and takes a white folded paper from his pocket. He offers it to her while looking down.

WASIULLAH. तेरे लिए . . .

Susanna doesn't take it. He looks up at her. She smiles, he smiles back.

Cut to:

Int. Wasiullah's house—bedroom Later.

SONG: तेरे लिए

WASIULLAH.
तेरे लिए तेरे लिए
लफ़्ज़ों में लम्हों की डोलियाँ लाए हैं
शेरों में ख़ुशबू की बोलियाँ लाए हैं
हमने सौ सौदे किए
तेरे लिऐ तेरे लिए . . .

Wasiullah sits at Susanna's feet on the bed, reciting a poem through which he seeks to ask her forgiveness for his deeds. He takes a vow to be like a lamb in her embrace or a butterfly in her palms. He finishes the recitation. Looking at him with admiring and forgiving eyes, she comes up to him and hugs him tenderly. He embraces her and closes his eyes.

Tere Liye—montage.

As Susanna sits in the garden in the cold, having her morning tea, Wasiullah tenderly drapes a shawl around her.

Wasiullah then carefully ties a scarf around Susanna's head.

In the kitchen Susanna stands in the corner as Wasiullah prepares goshtaba for her. He brings in a spoonful to get her approval. She hesitantly takes a bite and smiles. Scooping out a spoonful she too lovingly feeds him a bite.

At a small Mushaira, as the poet recites a poem, they make eye contact and smile at each other. Things seem to be getting back to normal for the couple.

Int. Bedroom. Later.

They are naked in bed. He is necking her with his eyes closed. He opens his eyes and looks at her. A moment later he suddenly slaps her hard.

Cut to:

Int. Dining room. Same.

Bringing Susanna her morning cup of tea, Maggie recoils, mortified at the condition of her face. Saying nothing, she backs away.

Goonga, across the room, catches her eye. Maggie gestures at him, signalling her horror. He nods, his single good eye flashing with anger.

Int. Parlour. Later.

In a corner of the lavishly furnished parlour, Susanna rolls out a prayer rug and faces east.

She carefully adjusts the folds of her naqab, then begins performing the namaz, her voice low and melodious.

Int. Bathroom. Later.

Susanna removes her naqab, drops it in a hamper and slams

the lid down. Then she wraps herself in a flowing robe, puts on some lipstick, and exits.

Int. Bedroom. Night.

In the corner of the room Wasiullah sits alone with his drink on the table. He caresses his cat as Mehdi Hassan's ghazal 'यह धुआँ सा' *plays on the casette recorder. Susanna enters quietly and walks towards him. He feels her presence, looks at her and smiles with eyes full of alcohol and affection. Susanna smiles back with more affection. Guilt flickers in Wasiullah's eyes.*

WASIULLAH. देख तो दिल के जान से उठता है . . .

Susanna drops her robe as Wasiullah looks away. She sits down next to him. She brushes his hair gently; he looks back at her with more love. He goes for his whisky glass but she picks the glass up before him. She takes a sip. Wasiullah smiles gently.

WASIULLAH. ये धुआँ-सा कहाँ से उठता है . . .

She suddenly slaps him hard. He is shocked for a moment but then smiles back. Another hard slap. He smiles with greater compassion this time. He asks for the whisky glass but she takes her hand away, nodding seductively. He tries again but Susanna gets up and begins to walk. Wasiullah follows her, still smiling. She reaches the end of the wall next to the mirror, Wasiullah is now very close to her. She takes a sip from the glass while looking at him invitingly. Wasiullah whispers into her ears.

WASIULLAH. इश्क़ एक मीर भारी पत्थर है कब यह तुझ नतावान से उठा है . . .

Wasiullah raises his eyebrows.

WASIULLAH. नतावान . . . माने . . .?

As she shakes her head to say that she doesn't know the answer, he suddenly slaps her hard and whispers in a choking voice.

WASIULLAH. कमज़ोर . . .

Susanna looks at Wasiullah seductively. He laughs; she giggles.
    The camera pans to the window. Outside, on a snow-covered hill, three figures are visible, toiling with picks and shovels.

Ext. Hillside. Continuous.

Bundled up in heavy clothing, working by lantern light, the Goonga, Ghalib and Maggie are digging a grave.
Cut to:

Ext. Campfire. Night.

Arun stares open-mouthed at his three drinking companion.

ARUN. फिर . . .

MAGGIE. फिर क्या . . . मुसाफ़िर सफ़र पे . . .

All three laugh.

ARUN. कहाँ . . .?

GHALIB. अपनी तलाश में . . .

They start singing a verse of Wasiullah's poems while Goonga tries to beat time on a wooden stool.
    Arun, aghast at the devilish nonchalance of his friends, gets up and throws the wooden stool.

ARUN. पागल हो गये हो तुम लोग!!

They stop and stare at him.

ARUN. उसे जान से मारने की क्या ज़रूरत थी . . . छोड़ देतीं साहेब उन्हें . . . वापस आ जातीं . . .

GHALIB (*smiling*). साहेब बचपन से school पैदल जाया करती थीं . . . दो रास्ते थे पहुंचने के, दोनों बराबर, न एक छोटा न दूसरा बड़ा . . . फिर जाने कहाँ से उस रास्ते पे एक कुता, थोड़ा पागल–सा रोज़ आकर उन्हें डराने लगा—भँऊ . . . गररर . . . भँऊ . . . वो चाहतीं तो दूसरे रास्ते को अपना लेतीं . . . पर उन्होंने बड़े साहब की छोटी पिस्तौल बस्ते में छुपाई और ढैं! . . . साहेब रास्ता नहीं बदला करतीं . . . कुत्ते का भेजा उड़ा देती हैं! . . . बचपन से . . .

The mood goes somber as Arun stares at Ghalib.
Cut to:

Ext. Hillside. Day.

Slanting sunlight and a cold blue sky.
   The poet's cat makes its way up a fresh mound of dirt in the gleaming, white snow. It paws the ground, sniffing, and meows.

Fade to black.

INTERVAL
Fade in:

Super—अमर प्रेम

Ext. Race track. Day.

Thundering hooves flash by as a dozen thoroughbreds gallop to the finish line! A large crowd in the stands is cheering. It's a close race—but a magnificent bay stallion pulls away and wins by half a length.

Ext. Winner's circle. Same.

The winning rider guides the horse through an applauding throng of well-wishers. The jockey, in colourful red and black silks, lifts his goggles: it's Goonga.

In the viewing gallery, Susanna softly smiles, wearing a huge sun hat. At 39, she's as beautiful as ever.

Ext. Winner's circle. Later.

Susanna poses, holding the reins of the winning horse. Still in the saddle, Goonga flashes a victory grin.

Susanna signals for Arun to come and stand next to her for the photograph. Over this, the voice of the track announcer:

ANNOUNCER. The winner's trophy goes to Qismat. His fourth victory in the last six races.

Ext. Stage inside the racecourse. Same.

On stage, the announcer has the microphone.

ANNOUNCER. Would Qismat's owner, the lovely Susanna Anna-Marie Johannes, please join me on stage?

Susanna walks amidst thunderous applause.

ANNOUNCER. To do the honours, let me call our esteemed guest of honour. Ladies and gentlemen, please welcome Mr Nikolai Vronsky, science attaché to the Russian consulate in Madras.

A big, handsome Russian in his forties walks on to the stage. He takes the trophy and speaks into the microphone.

VRONSKY. Namaste . . . I was just told that 'Qismat' means destiny, so I thank my 'Qismat' for the win.

VRONSKY. Moreover, I compliment the beautiful and gracious Susanna Johannes, for doing such wonders with her horse. Yes, people, I placed a bet on Qismat and did very well, thank you very much!

He pats his pockets. Laughter and more applause as he hands the trophy to Susanna and shakes her hand.

VRONSKY. I am Vronsky . . . Nikolai Vronsky.

SUSANNA. This is Anna . . .

He looks at her with surprise, still holding her hand.

VRONSKY. I don't believe it.

Susanna smiles flirtatiously.

SUSANNA. 'Qismat' . . .

He bends down to kiss her hand. In the crowd, Arun, Goonga and Ghalib look at each other with concern.
Cut to:

Ext. Racecourse arena. Later.

Vronsky and Susanna slowly walk through the racecourse and the crowds.

VRONSKY. Vronsky! Yes! नाम *maishoor* है बहोत . . .

SUSANNA. Maishoor . . . What . . .?

VRONSKY. (*struggling with the words*) Maishoor . . . Famous . . .

Susanna laughs at the Russian's attempt at Hindi.

SUSANNA Oh! . . . मशहूर . . .

He also smiles.

VRONSKY. But Anna . . . हिंदोस्तान में . . .अद्भुत . . .

SUSANNA. Anna Karenina is my favourite character . . .

He interrupts her mid-sentence.

VRONSKY. हिंदी में . . . कृपया . . . मैं हिंदी सीख रहा हूँ . . .

He pulls out a Russian-to-Hindi pocket dictionary. Susanna giggles.

SUSANNA. और क्या क्या सीखा है आपने हिंदी में?

VRONSKY. मैं आपसे अमर प्रेम करता हूँ . . .
Cut to:

Ext. Racecourse parking lot. Continuous.

They reach the parking lot, where Arun, Goonga and Ghalib are waiting with her car. Goonga nudges Arun to fetch her without delay.
    Arun reaches them.

ARUN. साहेब चलें . . .?

Susanna looks at Arun.

SUSANNA. Mr Vronsky—meet my little pal here, Arun.

Vronsky shakes Arun's hand, but sees Susanna leaving.

VRONSKY. Hey . . . Anna . . .

Arun whispers to himself at this address made by him.

ARUN (*astonished whisper*). Anna . . .!

Vronsky catches up.

VRONSKY. एक अति सुंदर भोजनालय में आज रात्रि आप कृपया मेरे साथ भोजन करें . . . मैं धनी हूँ बहोत . . .

Vronsky then pulls out a bundle of cash from his pocket. Susanna laughs aloud.

SUSANNA. What . . .?

He shuts his eyes in irritation.

VRONSKY. I would like to spend this play money on a nice dinner somewhere . . .?

She looks at him and smiles.

SUSANNA. Sorry, Mr Vronsky. I have some prior engagement.

She walks further; he follows.

VRONSKY. I can understand that. Can I at least drop you आपके निवास तक . . .

She has reached her car. Ghalib opens the front door for her.

SUSANNA. मेरे पास car है . . .

VRONSKY. और मेरे पास माँ है . . .

He looks down at the car. Everyone follows his gaze. The tyre of the car is flat.

VRONSKY. Amitabh Bachchan . . . *Deewar* . . .
Destiny . . .

Cut to:

Ext. Parking lot. Later.

The big black embassy car with a Russian flag up front leaves with Vronsky and Susanna inside.
    Ghalib, meanwhile, changes the tyre while an angry Goonga gestures for Arun to bend down. Arun refuses.

ARUN मेरी क्या ग़लती है इसमें . . .?

Goonga asks again with more authority this time.
    Arun bends down and Goonga smacks him hard on the back of his head.

Cut to:

Int. Arun's room. Night.

Arun is up late, his nose in a biology textbook. The door opens and Susanna comes in wearing a big white Russian ushanka (fur cap), holding a Vodka bottle in one hand and a big fat Hindi-to-Russian dictionary in the other.

SUSANNA (*in Russian*). Good evening . . .

Arun looks at her and sighs: 'Not again.' Susanna slides the dictionary on top of his biology book and removes the bottle of Campa Cola from his table.

SUSANNA. आज से no English or Campa Cola—only Russian and Vodka.

She pours herself some vodka.

ARUN. Russian और मैं . . . किसलिए . . .?

Susanna raises the glass for a toast.

SUSANNA (*in Russian*). Cheers . . .! क्यूँकि तुम Russia जा रहे हो . . . Moscow Medical Academy में पढ़ने.

ARUN. क्यूँ . . .!

She gulps the drink from her glass and gives him a peck on his cheek.

SUSANNA. क्यूँकि Nik loves me and I love you . . . my little Sugar . . .

ARUN. Nik!! उफ्फ़ . . . मुझे नहीं जाना Moscow Foscow . . .

Susanna pours another drink and offers it to Arun.

SUSANNA. क्यूँ . . .?

ARUN. क्यूँकि I hate vodka.

Susanna smiles mischievously and nods.

SUSANNA. नहीं . . . क्यूँकि you are jealous of Russians.

She laughs and gulps the vodka. Arun tosses the dictionary on to the bed and goes back to his biology book.
Cut to:

Int. Susanna's house. Night.

A festive dinner is in full swing. Seated at the piano, Vronsky sings the old Hindi film song—Raj Kapoor's 'आवारा हूँ'.
  At the bar, Susanna sips vodka as other guests applaud Vronsky's performance.

Int. Susanna's living room. Night.

SONG: Darling

A Russian folk dance number. Vronsky and Susanna, dressed as native Russians, dance about while other guests join in. Everyone is high on alcohol.

Susanna spots Arun coming downstairs and quietly making his way through the living room. She pulls him into the dance.

Vronksy and Susanna hold his hands and begin to dance in a circle in traditional Russian fashion. The song ends and Arun tries to smile as Susanna hooks her arm around his neck.

SUSANNA (*to Vronksy*). Nik . . . I need to confess something here . . .

Vronsky bows down.

SUSANNA. I am cheating on you . . .

Laughter from the guests. Vronsky raises his glass.

VRONSKY. मैं भी . . .

SUSANNA. Seriously . . . you know . . . I love him—he is my soulmate . . .

More laughter from the gathering.

VRONSKY. हे राम . . . मैं अग्नि हूँ . . .

Everyone looks at him with questioning eyes.

VRONSKY. I am burning . . .

Everyone laughs.

VRONSKY. I'll kill you, Arun.

Susanna smiles and looks at Arun.

SUSANNA. He's going to be your best man at our wedding . . .

VRONSKY. ये कभी नहीं हो सकता है . . .

He holds his hand up against his forehead like an old Hindi film heroine.

SUSANNA. Arun, you'll do it, won't you . . .?

Arun blushes.

ARUN I've never been . . . मतलब मुझे पता नहीं क्या करना होगा . . .

Susanna looks at him with eyes full of affection and alcohol.

SUSANNA. कुछ नहीं . . . बस . . . kiss करना होगा मुझे . . . यूँ . . .

She gives him a long, loving kiss. Whoops and cheers from the gathering. Vronsky laughs his heart out at Arun's discomfort.
    Suddenly Vronsky's satellite phone rings. He pats Susanna on the shoulder as he hurries off to take the call.

VRONSKY. Don't suck him dead, Anna.

This gets another laugh. Susanna wanders away, leaving Arun, whose face is red with embarrassment.

Cut to:

Ext. Lake pier. Night.

Vronksy talks to someone in Russian on his satellite phone while standing on the pier. His tone is warm, caring.

He turns to see Susanna standing there, listening. Vronsky is surprised. He hurriedly finishes his conversation and clicks off the phone.

VRONSKY. You left all the guests inside alone . . .?

SUSANNA. किससे बात कर रहे थे . . .?

VRONSKY. Hmmm . . . ! Moscow में एक colleague.

SUSANNA लड़की . . .?

Vronsky brushes a lock of her hair away from her forehead.

VRONSKY. तुमको क्या लगता है . . .?

SUSANNA. Your last words meant 'Darling, मैं जल्दी वापस आ रहा हूँ . . .

Vronsky looks away. Susanna comes closer.

SUSANNA. तुम मुझसे कुछ छुपा रहे हो Nik . . .

He turns back to her.

VRONSKY. No . . .

SUSANNA. Sure?

VRONSKY. No . . .

They look at each other in silence.
Cut to:

Int. Bedroom. Night.

Vronsky takes out a file emblazoned with a red cross and

a warning in Russian: 'TOP SECRET'. Vronsky hands it to her.

VRONSKY. मैं जब कन्याकुमारी जाती हूँ . . . जाता हूँ . . . तो कन्याकुमारी नहीं जाता . . .

He looks at her; she raises her eyebrow.

VRONSKY. मैं Koodankulam जाता हूँ . . .

SUSANNA (*whispering*). Koodankulam . . .

VRONSKY. Yes . . .

She unties a ribbon on the secret file and opens it. On the first page the words 'PROJECT KOODANKULAM' in big, bold letters. The next page has a diagram of a large and complicated machine. Caption: 'VVER 1000-Reactor'.

VRONSKY. We are helping your government—of course, secretly—to set up the development of light water reactor technology in India.

Susanna goes through the file but can't make any sense of it.

SUSANNA. What's that supposed to mean . . .?

Vronsky takes a deep breath, and looks out of the window.

VRONSKY. Soon your country is going to be a self-sufficient nuclear state. एक परमाणु सक्षम राज्य . . .

The last page of the file has a photograph of Indian scientists, with some Russian delegates and Vronsky.

SUSANNA. Nik . . . तुम जासूस हो?

VRONSKY. नहीं दोस्त हूँ और आपसे अमर प्रेम करता हूँ . . .

The music of 'Star News' from the year 1998 plays on the soundtrack.

Cut to:

Int. Living Room. Day.

The music continues on the TV screen as the headlines are read out by Prannoy Roy.
    The angle widens to capture a football match on the lawn outside the stables.

Cut to:

Ext. Ground outside the stables. Day.

A match between the syces and the stable boys. Arun and Vronsky are duelling in a mean hardcore dribble, but Arun is no match for Vronsky, who tackles him easily.

VRONSKY (*while dribbling*). तुम्हारा क्या गया जो तुम रोते हो? तुम क्या लाए थे जो तुमने खो दिया . . .?

Vronsky winks. Arun tries to take the ball, but Vronsky dodges him again.

VRONSKY. परिवर्तन संसार का नियम है . . .

Vronksy dodges him. He drives for the goal. He kicks the ball into the goal. He leaps up and slaps a high-five with his teammates. He walks over to the dejected Arun and puts a hand on his shoulder.

VRONSKY. मेरा तेरा, छोटा बड़ा, मन से मिटा दो, फिर सब तुम्हारा है और तुम सब के हो . . . मैं India का हूँ और तुम रूस के. बेटा अर्जुन . . .

He looks into Arun's eyes and smiles.

Cut to:

Int. Living room. Night.

Arun, dressed up as a native Russian, dances with Susanna and Vronsky.

Ext. Campfire. Night.

The same dance is being performed by Ghalib, Maggie and Goonga. They are also dressed in traditional Russian clothes.

Russian arrival—montage.

ARUN (*voice-over*). India का nuclear test successful हुआ और Hiroshima बना मेरा दिल। दो bomb फेंके साहेब ने एक साथ, पहला शादी का और दूसरा मुझे रूस रवाना करने का।

The music continues into the following visuals. Arun's aircraft lands at the Moscow airport. Arun travels in a cab on the snowy roads of Moscow.

Int. Arun's bathroom. Night.

The present day. Holding a toothbrush Nandini is staring at her husband, astonished. She speaks with a lot of toothpaste foam in her mouth.

NANDINI (*astonished*). That's how you went to Medical School in Moscow . . . ! पहले क्यूँ नहीं बताया ये मुझे।

ARUN. क्यूँकि वहाँ जो हुआ . . . Nik के साथ . . . बताने के लायक नहीं था . . .

NANDANI. वो भी . . .? कैसे . . .?

Arun looks up towards the sky.

ARUN. किस्मत . . .

Int. Moscow Medical Academy—anatomy class. Day.

Ten corpses, wrapped in cotton shrouds, are stretched out on the lab tables. Arun is one of twenty medical students standing alongside, listening, as a lecturer explains the purpose of the coming dissection (MOS).

Arun's gaze drifts down to the body lying before him, with his mouth open.

ARUN (*voice-over*). इस बार ग़लती मेरी थी . . . मुझे अपना मुँह बंद रखना चाहिए था . . .

Ext. Ukraine. Coffee Shop. Day.

A group of medical students are having an intellectual discussion in a local coffee shop in a small suburb of the Ukrainian capital, Kiev, with a few medical textbooks spread out on the table.

Arun is among them. He glances outside, then frowns.

ARUN (*voice-over*). कॉलेज में एक seminar trip पर मैं Ukraine गया था, और वहाँ जो नज़ारा मैंने देखा उससे मेरा होश फ़ाख़्ता हो गए . . .

At a street corner, Arun see the Vronsky family walking along—a happy bunch.

He stares in dismay at the kids licking ice-cream cones. Vronsky stands by, holding their mylar balloons as his wife daubs at their faces with Vronsky's handkerchief.

Arun snaps a photo with his mobile phone.

ARUN (*voice-over*). हरामज़ादे Vronsky के पास एक नहीं दो Anna थीं . . . एक India में और दूसरी Ukraine में . . . मैं आज तक ख़ुद को उसकी मौत का ज़िम्मेदार मानता हूँ . . . मुझे वो तस्वीर साहेब को नहीं भेजनी चाहिए थी . . .

Ext. Chapel. Night.

CLANG! CLANG! Susanna is ringing the bell again. Six silhouetted women in robes swirl around the chapel, casting ominous shadows as they dance about.

A close shot of Jesus on the cross shows real tears running down his face.

Ext. Driveway. Dusk.

A taxi arrives and Vronsky gets out. Ghalib emerges from the house. Goonga wrestles with two big suitcases up the front steps, muttering incomprehensibly.

VRONSKY. Anna कहाँ है . . .?

GHALIB. Market going . . .

VRONSKY. किस लिए . . .?

Maggie emerges from inside and takes his briefcase and coat.

MAGGIE. New wedding gown लाने . . .

Vronsky is confused. All three suddenly burst into laughter. Vronsky tries to smile but is confused.

Cut to:

Int. Living room. Dusk.

Vronsky lies on his stomach on a big wooden cot as Goonga walks barefoot on his bare back, giving him a massage. Ghalib and Maggie are showing him photographs from an old album.

GHALIB. This Major—first husband.

VRONSKY. Handsome chap . . . He was killed by the panther, I believe . . .

Goonga sits astride Vronksy's back, as if in the saddle. He leans forward and grunts in a monstrous whisper, while massaging Vronsky's neck.

GHALIB. चुप साले गूंगे . . .

Vronsky is curious.

VRONSKY. What did he say . . .?

GHALIB. He saying कि we धक्का मारो Major . . . back से . . . फिर panther eat him.

Goonga laughs out loud monstrously. He is joined by Maggie. Vronsky is confused again. Ghalib consoles him.

GHALIB. No, sir . . . He is पागल . . . Don't सुनो him, sir . . . He is झूठा number 1.

He brings out the photograph of Jimmy and his guitar.

GHALIB. Husband number 2, Jimmy—very good song, sir . . .

He starts to sing one of Jimmy's songs. Goonga mumbles again. Ghalib stops singing and glares at him.

GHALIB. गूंगे साले चुप कर . . .

Vronsky is even more curious.

VRONSKY. What . . .?

GHALIB. Nothing, sir . . . Mad . . .

This time Maggie speaks.

MAGGIE. They say, sir, कि हमने पहले उसे heroin का overdose दिया and then dragged him to क़बरिस्तान.

She pretends to inject herself.

Nervous now, Vronsky gets up and starts to put on his shirt. Ghalib shows him another photograph.

GHALIB. Husband number 3 . . . We खोदो one grave in snow and गाड़ो him ज़िंदा . . . ज़िंदा . . .

He mockingly performs the whole action of digging a grave. Vronsky reacts as he hears the chapel bells tolling.
All three servants laugh like maniacs. Vronsky walks off, but Maggie takes out the Vronsky family picture and blocks his way.
She giggles as Vronsky's face turns pale with fear.
Vronsky's focus shifts from the photograph to Susanna, in black, standing at the door.

SUSANNA. This is you, my पति परमेश्वर number 4, with his अर्धांगिनी number 2.

Maggie, Goonga and Ghalib start to sing from behind.

TRIO (*singing*). चार चार चार चार . . .

Vronksy picks up his briefcase while muttering.

VRONSKY. You are all crazy . . . This is a mad house and I am getting out of here . . .

SUSANNA. Not without this.

She takes the 'TOP SECRET' file from the briefcase lying on the table. Its lock has been ripped away. Goonga, Ghalib and Maggie start dancing around Vronsky.

TRIO (*singing*). Darling, आँखों से आँखें चार करने दो, रोको ना, रोको ना, मुझको प्यार करने दो . . .

VRONSKY. Anna . . . please . . . I can explain . . . let's talk.

He walks towards her but she retreats.

Ext. Back garden. Night.

Susanna comes into the garden, pursued by Vronsky, who has tears in his eyes. He is trailed by Maggie, Ghalib and Goonga.

VRONSKY. Come on, honey, she's not my wife . . . She's my colleague, an agent . . .

SUSANNA. Ah! And you? A double agent . . .?

Vronsky avoids this one.

VRONSKY. हम husband–wife की acting कर रहे थे!

They are at the edge of the Naag Temple as Susanna holds the file.

SUSANNA. मैं जानती हूँ कि तुम एक बोहुत अच्छा husband play कर सकते हो लेकिन इतना अच्छा daddy play करना no chance.

VRONSKY (*hesitantly*). You're so wrong, Anna, you're so wrong.

SUSANNA. Always . . .

A mocking smile spreads over her face and she tosses the file into the pit. Vronsky goes after it. Climbing down the thick rope ladder.

VRONSKY. I'll quit the job, honey, and I'll be back for you—forever. मैं आपसे अमर प्रेम करता हूँ . . .

Vronsky is disappearing into the shadows unaware that he's passing snakes.
   At the bottom, he picks up his file and screams.

Up above, Susanna walks away followed by her trio.

Fade to black.

Super—प्यार की क़ीमत

Ext. Naag Temple. day.

Some uniformed local policemen and Russian embassy officials are peering over the edge into the pit. In the background, various servants and syces watch as one of the cops cranks a winch, lifting Vronsky's dead body into the sunlight. It's stiff and still draped with snakes.

Someone gives the rope a shake, dumping the snakes back into the pond below. SPLASH!

Int. Police station. Day.

Surrounded by common criminals, beggars and other street folk, Susanna sits on a bench in the Panchgani police station. She's staring at the floor, lost in bleak thoughts.

An assistant inspector comes up.

ASSISTANT INSPECTOR. चलिए, बुलाया है . . .

Int. DCP's office. Day

A cop in plain clothes escorts Susanna inside an office, where a few Russian officials-sip coffee with some Indian plain clothes and uniformed officials. They stop talking and look at Susanna in silence.

She is escorted to an adjacent room. Another officer in a safari suit stands facing the window, looking outside, and going through some papers in a file. He signals to the officer to leave the room. The officer looks at Susanna and leaves the room.

OFFICER. बैठिए . . .

He turns. It is Keemat Lal, now a serious and elegant senior officer in a dark safari suit and a pair of aviators nestled on his nose. He takes off his glasses and smiles.

KEEMAT. कैसी हैं . . . मादाम . . .

It takes a moment for Susanna to recognize him.

SUSANNA. आप . . .

KEEMAT. जी . . . मै . . . क़ीमत . . .

SUSANNA. Inspector . . .

KEEMAT. Assistant Commissioner of Police . . . ACP, Keemat Lal, Intelligence Bureau.

He hands her his business card.

KEEMAT. कैसी हैं आप . . .?

Before she can answer:

KEEMAT. कहाँ फँस गयी हैं . . . इस बार . . .

SUSANNA. देखिए . . . क़ीमत जी . . .

KEEMAT. जी नहीं . . . क़ीमत बस . . .

Keemat smiles and continues.

KEEMAT. Reports पढ़ी हैं मैंने . . . local officer आपका भारी दुश्मन जान पड़ता है . . . सारे शक़ सबूत में बदल रखे हैं . . . मैंने तो ना पहले माना था, ना ही अब मानने को तैयार हूँ कि आप किसी को . . . ख़ामख़ाह . . . ख़ैर . . . Foreign Ministry . . . Russian Embassy . . . case पेचीदा . . . ऐसा भी नहीं मगर . . . आप तो समझदार . . . लेकिन इस बार . . . चलिए मैं तो हूँ . . .

Susanna looks at him blankly. He clears his throat, and leans forward.

KEEMAT. एक चीज़ missing है आपके पति के सामान से . . . वो अगर मिल जाती तो मेरे हाथ थोड़े से . . . आप समझ रही हैं ना . . .?

Susanna takes out the 'TOP SECRET' files from her bag and keeps it on the table. Keemat giggles.

KEEMAT. बस . . . अब आप मुझ पर . . . क्या बात है . . . ! वैसे शाम को . . . मसरूफ़ होंगी . . . नहीं मुझे मौका-ए-वारदात का मुआयना . . . ख़ैर . . . कभी और . . .

SUSANNA. आप veg. हैं कि non-veg. . . .?

Keemat giggles again . . .

KEEMAT. आप भी . . . non-veg. . . .

SUSANNA. पीना क्या पसंद करेंगे . . .?

KEEMAT. अरे . . . भाई . . . वैसे . . . आप क्या लेती हैं . . .?

SUSANNA. Vodka के अलावा सब कुछ . . .

Keemat bursts into laughter and suddenly covers his mouth, so the officials outside don't hear him.

KEEMAT. मरवाएंगी आप मुझे . . . मादाम . . .

She looks at him sharply.

KEEMAT. Sorry . . . सुनैना . . .

She smiles.
Cut to:

Int. Dining room. Night.

Susanna sits across from Keemat Lal at her dining table. They have had quite a lot to drink. Ghalib and Maggie are clearing the dessert plates and empty wine bottles.

SUSANNA. K . . . have some liquor . . .

She starts to pour some into his glass. He bends forward.

KEEMAT. अरे नहीं भाई . . . सुनो तो . . . सुनैना . . .

SUSANNA. ये तो पीना ही होगा . . . मेरे father का favourite brand . . . आपको देख कर उनकी बहुत याद आती है . . .

KEEMAT. Father की . . .?

SUSANNA. Very precise . . . Every inch the proper gentleman.

A flattered Keemat studies a full-length portrait of Susanna's father on the wall. She touches his hand for a moment while giving him the whisky.

KEEMAT. एक बार देखा था मैंने . . . बहुत साल पहले, racecourse में आप भी थीं . . . नन्हीं सी . . . बड़े फूलों वाली frock में, गुलाबी रंग की . . . काले जूते, आँखों पे कत्थई चश्मा . . . और सर पे बादलों का गोल बड़ा top—आहा . . . देवी लग रही थी . . . बस चलता तो आपका मंदिर बनवा देता

She looks at him again. He fumbles.

KEEMAT. नहीं . . . वो church का तो मुझे पता नहीं . . . कोई objection ले ले तो . . .

She bursts out laughing. She smiles at his boyish foolishness.

He places his hand inside his jacket pocket and pulls out a vial. Casually, he takes out a blue pill from the bottle. He pops it into his mouth and washes it down with a big gulp of his drink.

Cut to:

Ext. Naag Temple. Night.

Under a starry sky, Susanna leans against a tree as Keemat Lal has a look at the snake pit.

KEEMAT (*leaning over*). काफी गहरा है . . . अंधेरे में कोई भी फिसल के गिर सकता है . . .

SUSANNA. उस दिन पूरे चाँद की रात थी . . . और और वो गिरा नहीं . . . उतरा था अपने आप . . .

KEEMAT (*surprised*). Oohh . . . बारिश में सीढ़ियों पे फिसलन होगी . . . काई भी . . .

Susanna flirtatiously shakes her head.

SUSANNA. बारिश और इस मौसम में . . .

KEEMAT. तो फिर शराब के नशे में तो कुछ भी हो जाता है . . .

SUSANNA. उन दिनों छोड़ रखी थी उसने . . . शराब . . .

Keemat helplessly looks at her.

KEEMAT. अब या तो . . .? फिर कैसे . . .? क्या कहूँ . . .?

Susanna looks at him in all innocence.

SUSANNA. छोड़िए . . .

KEEMAT. हैं . . .?

They look at each other in silence as the crickets sing in the night.

Int. Susanna's bedroom. Night.

Keemat Lal is naked in Susanna's bed, semi-delirious as she sits astride him, pinning his hands down on the bed and grinding away.

KEEMAT. मादाम . . . अंधेरा . . . घुप्प घना घनघोर, वर्षा ऋतु की मदमस्त मूसलाधार तूफ़ानी बारिश, नशे में गोरा गिर गया . . . मर गया . . . चुक गया . . . मा–दा–म . . .!

Cut to:

Ext. Driveway. Day.

Ready to leave, a shaved and showered Keemat Lal opens the door of his official jeep. Hesitating, he waves at Susanna. He starts to climb in but he walks back to her.

KEEMAT. आपका ये एहसान मैं ज़िंदगी भर नहीं चुका पाऊंगा . . . ऐसा सुख और संतोष, जैसे गंगा नहा के आया हूँ . . . अब बेफ़िक्र रहिए आप . . . और दिल्ली आएं कभी तो याद कीजिएगा . . .

Susanna smiles. He smiles back.

KEEMAT. जाऊँ . . .?

Susanna speaks with a firm nod.

SUSANNA. जी . . .!

He turns back and walks towards his jeep. Arun's voice-over continues.

ARUN (*voice-over*). Keemat जाने के लिए नहीं, आने के लिए गया था . . . वो दिल्ली पहुँचा जरूर पर अपना दिल यहीं छोड़ गया . . .

Ext. Driveway. Day.

Keemat's jeep roars down the driveway. He has a big bouquet in his lap.

ARUN (*voice-over*). बार-बार वापस लेने की नीयत से आता, पर हर बार फिर वहीं भूल जाता . . .

Int. Susanna's bedroom/study. Day.

Susanna reads Anna Karenina *sitting in the courtyard. Maggie arrives.*

MAGGIE. मादाम . . . चलिए . . .

Susanna looks at Maggie and closes her book in anger.

Cut to:

Int. Living room. Day.

Another day. Susanna in a different outfit enters the living room. Keemat is popping a blue pill and washing it down with a glass of water. He notices Susanna walking in. He freezes in his tracks and slyly hides the pill bottle behind him while he displays a stuffed toy for her and smiles.

A visibly nervous Keemat straightens up as Susanna walks up to him. She grabs the bottle from his hand and he smiles sheepishly.

ARUN (*voice-over*). और फिर Keemat का आना, आता ही रहा.

Int. Bedroom. Night.

Susanna looks at the ceiling with cold, blank eyes as a bare-bodied Keemat lies on top of her, with his eyes closed, smiling contentedly.

On the bedside table is a small white vial with its lid off—the label reads 'Viagra'.

ARUN (*voice-over*). साहेब के पास कोई option भी नहीं था और Keemat के सुख और संतोष की सीमाएं भी तो अब बढ़ती ही जा रही थीं . . .

Int. Bedroom. Night.

Keemat cries like a child as Susanna looks at him blankly.

KEEMAT. नहीं नहीं नहीं . . . किसी और ने नहीं, हमने खुद बताया मिसेज को . . .

He sobs, almost uncontrollably.

SUSANNA. पर क्यों . . .?

KEEMAT. हमें divorce चाहिए था . . .

Susanna is alarmed. Keemat takes out a paper from his pocket.

KEEMAT. और मिल भी गया . . . देखिए . . .

He hugs her and puts his wet face on her shoulder.

KEEMAT. आपके बिना जीना . . . मुमकिन नहीं है अब . . . समझ रही हैं ना आप . . . और फिर आपको भी तो मेरी जरूरत है . . .

He pulls out a cross, tied to a thin chain around his neck.

KEEMAT. Jesus की कसम . . .

Eyes wide, Susanna stares at the dangling crucifix.
Cut to:

Int. Chapel. Day.

Sunlight shines through the stained glass windows.

The chapel, adorned with floral garlands, is filled with dozens of cops—row after row of Keemat's friends, dressed in their uniforms, beaming at the joyful groom as he stands at the altar next to Susanna.

Her face is a mask, flawless and impassive.

As the local priest reads the marriage vows (MOS), Goonga leaps on the rope hanging down from the tower.

Ext/Int. Chapel. Day.

The bell swings and the familiar, incessant clanging begins.
A heavy rain starts falling.

PRIEST. Dear friends, after such a tragic accident we find ourselves questioning God. Why, we wonder, why must you take a good man from us . . .?

Keemat lies dead in his coffin as the same colleagues and friends mourn his death. Susanna stands expressionless.

Dissolve to:

Int. Susanna's bedroom. Day.

Priest's voice-over continues on the soundtrack.

We see a sweaty and exhausted Susanna lying naked under the sheets, looking up at the ceiling. Keemat is heaped on top of her, motionless.

As the warm summer breeze comes into the room, a curtain flutters and topples the vial placed on the bedside table with its lid open. Susanna watches as a bunch of blue pills spill on to the floor.

PRIEST (*voice-over*). . . . leaving such a devoted wife and partner? Is there no rhyme or reason to life? May his soul rest in peace. May God give you the peace of mind.

Int. Arun's bedroom—Mumbai. Night.

The present day. Arun and Nandini are side by side with the album propped up on her knees.

NANDINI. Oh my God! Viagra bottle में poison था . . .

ARUN. ना . . . Viagra bottle में Viagra ही था . . .

NANDINI. फिर . . .? (*realises—with a snicker in her tone*) Overdose . . .?

ARUN. Leading to a massive heart-attack . . . Very unfortunate . . . Terrible accident . . .

NANDINI. Accident? She killed him . . . तुम्हें पता था . . .

ARUN. अरे मुझे कैसे पता होता . . .?

Nandini nods and pulls his cheeks.

NANDINI. सच . . . तुम तो अंधे थे ना उसके प्यार में . . .

Arun smiles.

ARUN. अंधा तो था पर उनके नहीं किसी और के प्यार में . . .

She looks at him suspiciously.

NANDINI. Aha. Your darling Eva.
Cut to:

Ext. Solarium. Day.

A taxi arrives in the driveway of Susanna's estate with Eva, 28, a fresh-faced, pale, typical Russian girl looking out of the window. Arun is seated beside her.

At the porch Goonga, Ghalib and Maggie watch the taxi drive up.

GHALIB (*voice-over*). पूछ मत अपने साहेब का हाल . . .

Cut to:

Int. Living room. Night.

Everyone sits and drinks quietly in the living room which is decorated for New Year's Eve. A big cake lies ready to be cut on the dining table.

In the background, a television is tuned to a news channel.

Ghalib and Arun talk in whispers.

GHALIB. बड़े साहब के कमरे में रहने लगी हैं. अब . . . हफ्तों-हफ्तों बाहर नहीं निकलती हैं . . . देखो, शायद आज तेरे लिए आ जाएं बाहर . . .

Maggie comes down the stairs.

MAGGIE. कह रही हैं कि दस मिनट में आएंगी नीचे . . .

ARUN. तीन घंटे हो गए . . . कब होंगे उनके दस मिनट पूरे . . . क्या कर रही हैं . . .?

MAGGIE. पता नहीं . . .

ARUN. मतलब . . .? तुम फिर बाहर से वापस आ गयी . . .?

MAGGIE. I don't dare any more, man . . . परसों कोशिश की थी। ऐसे काँच का फूलदान फेंक के मारा . . . बाल-बाल बची मैं . . .

She leans forward.

MAGGIE. थोड़ी खिसक भी गयी है . . . ऊपर से . . . She's going nuts.

In the background, we hear a news reader on TV reading out loud—'The Government has struck a deal with the terrorists to free the hostages of IC-814 . . .'

Everyone turns towards the TV. But Arun picks up a gift-wrapped package and walks upstairs.

Cut to:

Int. Susanna's father's bedroom. Night.

Arun taps on the door, then cautiously enters. Most of the lights are out; a few candles illuminate the old-fashioned furniture. Horse and Hound prints hang on the walls, plus various regimental guns and animal-head trophies. A grandfather clock is ticking.

From the far corner, we hear a soft voice.

SUSANNA. Sugar . . . दरवाज़ा बंद कर दो . . .

ARUN. साहेब . . . इतने अंधेरे में क्यों बैठी हैं आप . . .?

SUSANNA. इस मौसम का उजाला चुभता है मुझे . . . Oh my, my . . . look at you . . . क्या बना दिया है दुनिया ने मेरे छोटे से खरगोश को . . .

ARUN. Happy New Year साहेब . . .

Arun hands over the gift to her, but she doesn't take it.

SUSANNA. कितने gift लाए हो Moscow से . . .?

He looks at her. A streak of jealousy flashes in Susanna's eyes. Arun smiles as Susanna turns.

SUSANNA. क्या नाम है . . .?

ARUN. Eva . . . गुस्सा हैं आप . . .?

SUSANNA. किससे ?

ARUN. मरी दोस्त से . . .

SUSANNA. उसकी तो शक्ल भी नहीं देखी है मैंने और ना ही देखने की ख़्वाहिश है . . .

She starts searching through her hair again.

ARUN. क्या, ढूँढ क्या रही हैं आप . . .?

SUSANNA. एक है कहीं छुपा हुआ . . . कमबख़्त जब भी ढूंढती हूँ गुम हो जाता है.

ARUN. सफ़ेद बाल . . .?

She puts her fingers on her lips.

SUSANNA. Shhh . . . चुप . . . it's a bad omen.

Arun puts the gift on the table and takes her hair in his hands. He finds the grey hair.

ARUN. ये रहा . . .

She smiles, with a feeling of comfort.

SUSANNA. देख कितनी जरूरत है मुझे तुम्हारी . . . कैंची देना . . .

She holds the hair as Arun gets the scissors from the dressing table.

SUSANNA. कितने साल बाद देख रहे हो तुम मुझे . . .?

ARUN. लगभग दो . . .

SUSANNA. कुछ बदली हूँ मैं . . .?

Arun raises the grey hair with his fingers.

ARUN. नहीं . . . वही gramophone, वही telephone, मोमबत्तियाँ, मसहरी, किसी museum की तरफ कभी जाइएगा नहीं, वरना चोरी हो जाएंगी। वैसे एक change तो आया है

She looks at him.

ARUN. हल्की सी और ख़ूबसूरत हो गई हैं आप . . . बस . . .

She smiles as he cuts the hair—snip! He stretches it, displaying it to her.

SUSANNA. वहाँ box में . . . कब से ख़त नहीं लिखा तुमने . . . अब समझी कि साहेब क्यों याद नहीं आती हैं तुम्हें . . .

Arun places the hair inside a cosmetic box that contains a few other long, grey hairs.

ARUN. पढ़ाई से फ़ुर्सत कहाँ मिलती है साहेब . . .

SUSANNA. झूठे . . .

As the clock strikes midnight, she heaves a sigh and moves to a tall oval mirror near the window. Outside, the sound of fireworks.

SUSANNA. I hate New Year's Eve.

Int. Living room. Night.

Toasts and greetings from everyone as a confused and slightly nervous Eva looks up at the staircase.

Cut to:

Int. Susanna's father's bedroom. Continuous.

She stands in front of the mirror.

SUSANNA. देखो तुम्हारा यह नया साल क्या करता है मेरे साथ . . . हर बार थोड़ा सा बदसूरत बना जाता है मुझे . . .

Arun follows her gaze as she inspects herself, full of doom.

SUSANNA. कोई सच नहीं बोलता है मेरे सामने . . . तुम्हारे सिवा . . . मैं बूढ़ी हो रही हूँ . . .?

Arun looks at her in silence.
Cut to:

Int. Outside Susanna's fathers bedroom. Continuous.

Eva walks up the wooden staircase.

Int. Susanna's father's bedroom. Same.

Susanna now faces Arun.

ARUN. बिल्कुल ग़लत . . . चेहरे से अब भी आप वही हैं . . . सालों पुरानी Miss साहेब.

She opens her robe and shows him her naked body.

SUSANNA. और बदन से . . .?

Appalled, Arun averts his gaze. He keeps his gaze fixed on a photo of young Susanna and her father.

SUSANNA. सच बताओ . . .

She holds her breasts.

SUSANNA. मैं सूखने लगी हूँ . . .?

He won't look at her.

SUSANNA. बड़े होकर शर्मीले हो गए हो . . . hmm छू के देखो . . .

Cupping her breasts, she walks to him.
Cut to:

Int. Outside Susanna's fathers bedroom. Continuous.

Eva stands at the door, trying to hear the conversation.

Int. Susanna's father's bedroom. Continuous.

As if on cue, a huge Black Widow spider climbs on to the cosmetic case! Arun's mouth falls open in fear.
  He watches as it makes its way towards the edge of the table. Susanna comes closer.

ARUN. साहेब नहीं . . .

SUSANNA. क्यों . . .? तुम्हारी हर पढ़ाई की जिम्मेदारी साहेब की है . . .

His gaze is fixed, as he grabs the gift-wrapped book and smashes the spider! Susanna shrieks. Eva steps back from the door.

SUSANNA. Sugar . . .

Susanna looks at the dead spider, Arun tears off the gift-wrapping paper, scrapes the squished thing on to a newspaper and makes for the door. He finds a shocked Eva outside. He pulls her by the arm and hurriedly exits.
  Inside, an emotionally wounded Susanna looks at the book, through the remains of the gift wrap paper. It's The Seven Wives of Bluebeard *by Anatole France.*
Cut to:

Ext. Arun's quarters. Day.

Eva opens the door to fetch the morning paper. As she reads the headlines—'IC-814 HOSTAGES RELEASED'—she notices a gift basket full of roses and a note kept on the footsteps below. She sits down on the front step.

EVA. Arun . . . Come look, she's sent a peace offering.

Arun is somewhere inside.

ARUN. She can go to hell.

Eva pulls away the tissue paper.

EVA. No . . . She says . . . 'Sweets to the sweet.'

In the middle of the basket is a cut crystal bowl of sugar cubes.

EVA. And the sugar cubes.

ARUN. Send it back . . .

EVA. No . . . it's really sweet of her . . .

As she lifts the sugar bowl, a black snake slithers forth! Eva screams as it slips past her bare feet. Instantly, Arun is there in his pyjamas, just in time to see the snake wriggling across the lawn.
Eva, her face beet red, is jumping up and down, shrieking.

Cut to:

Int. Susanna's house. Day.

Arun bursts through Susanna's door, brushing past Maggie, who's scrubbing the floor. He runs up the stairs.

Int. Susanna's bedroom. Moments later.

Arun runs down to the master bedroom. The door is open, the room is empty.

Int. Hallway. Same.

Maggie looks up to see Arun leaning over the upstairs railing.

ARUN. साहेब . . .?

She looks at his fuming eyes.
Cut to:

Ext. Stables. Day.

In the shadow of the barn, Arun finds Susanna sponging down one of her thoroughbreds. It's a hot day; she's rolled up the sleeves of her blouse. Her hair is loosely pulled back. Arun stops the horse by holding the reins.

ARUN. अब ख़ुश हैं आप . . .? वो Moscow जा रही है वापस . . .

Susanna smiles.

SUSANNA. मुबारक हो . . .

ARUN. आपको माफ़ी मांगनी होगी उससे . . .

She smiles more.

SUSANNA. फूलों के लिए . . .?

ARUN. नहीं . . . साँपों के लिए . . .

SUSANNA. Ah . . .! समझाओ उसे . . . ये India है . . . यहाँ चींटियों की तरह पाए जाते हैं साँप . . . चारो तरफ़.

Susanna dismounts and leads the horse towards the stables. Arun follows.

Int. Stables. Continuous.

A syce hurries up and takes the horse. Susanna hangs the bridle in the tack room.

ARUN. मै उससे शादी करना चाहता हूँ . . .

Susanna turns, looks at him and bursts into laughter.

SUSANNA. शादी करोगे . . . marraige that to with a Russian . . .! Gorbachev बना देगी तुम्हारा . . .

She tries to move away but Arun holds her by the arm.

ARUN. साहेब हर हद पार करती जा रही हैं आप . . . मजबूर मत कीजिए मुझे वर्ना पीछे पछताएंगी . . .

They look at each other in silence.

SUSANNA. पछता तो रही हूँ मैं . . .

She suddenly holds him by the hair, violently drags him inside and pushes him into the mound of manure.

SUSANNA. यहाँ से उठाया था तुझे . . . भूलना मत . . . अगली बार ज़बान उठाने से पहले यहाँ की खुशबुओं को याद कर लेना . . . मैं ना होती तो सारी ज़िंदगी यहीं घोड़े की लीद में सड़ते रहते . . . कई जनम गुज़र जाएंगे मेरा उधार चुकाने में . . .

ARUN. इसी जनम में चुकाऊंगा . . . आपका उधार . . . साहेब . . .

Arun walks past her and stands in front of Goonga who was listening to the conversation. Arun holds his hand and drags him away. Goonga is resistent, mumbling out loudly back at Susanna, still standing inside the stables.

Cut to:

Int. Arun's bedroom—Mumbai. Night.

The present day. Arun and Nandini are cuddled up on the bed. The lights are out.

NANDINI. So many secrets . . . My God, Arun . . . और कितनी girlfriends थीं तुम्हारी . . .?

ARUN. Eva ने पूरे college में साहेब के किस्से मशहूर कर दिए और फिर हर लड़की मेरे पास आने से कतराती थी . . . तुम्हें बता देता तो तुम भी शादी नहीं करती मुझसे . . .

Nandini shivers at the thought. She turns to him.

NANDINI. Thank God . . . अब ना किसी का डर . . . ना किसी का उधार . . .

She sees his mournful face.

NANDINI. You still miss her . . .? इस सबके बाद भी . . .? It's insane.

Arun tries a rueful smile but fails, touched Nandini kisses him.

NANDINI. सो जाओ . . . सुबह होने को है . . . and just don't let me catch you dreaming about her.

The camera moves in on Arun, whose eyes shine in the darkness. He is lost in thought.

Fade out.

Ext. Susanna's house. Day.

A grey, foggy day in Panchgani. Clouds are brooding over the heavily wooded hills.

The camera drifts down to the blackened remains of Susanna's house.

In a raincoat and hat, Arun is a lonely figure, poking through the ashes, taking in the devastation.

At length, he walks through the destroyed foyer and stands on the front steps.

On a hill directly opposite, he sees the chapel. And the motionless bell in the tower.

As he walks through the burnt remains something grabs his attention: an old photograph, half burnt. Arun picks up the photo and wipes it clean of debris.

Cut to:

Insert.

It's the picture of Susanna as a young girl, holding hands with her father on the beach in Goa.

Cut to:

Int. Arun's apartment—Mumbai. Night.

Nandini clears the dinner things from in front of the aged Goonga, who is finishing his coffee. Little Aditya is there too, but his supper is untouched.

NANDINI (*to Aditya*). I'm warning you. Hot or cold, it makes no difference, you eat something or I'm calling your father.

Nandini shows him the cellphone. Aditya looks at Goonga, and they both suddenly burst into laughter. Nandini presses the green button on the cellphone.

But on the phone, she hears a recording: 'This user's telephone is currently not in service. Please try again later.'

Dissolve to:

Int. Arun's apartment. Later.

Nandini sits at the desk, checking her laptop for emails. Nothing.

She goes to the website of a Mumbai hotel, then dials their number.

NANDINI. Hello, yes . . . Mr Arun Kumar, please. (*Pause.*) No, please check again. He arrived last night, with the Criminal Forensics group. (*Pause.*) I see . . . No, thanks very much.

Cut to:

Int. Arun apartment. Day.

Nandini cries as Chetna tries to console her.

CHETNA. Come on, Nandi . . . It'll be fine . . . I've a friend in Vodafone. He is finding out. अभी पता चल जायेगा कि last phone उसने कहाँ से किया था . . . चुप हो जाओ . . . लो . . . पानी लो.

Nandini tries to sip the water as Aditya skips into the room holding Nandini's phone.

ADITYA. It's Daddy . . . I told him कि तुम बहोत गुस्से में हो . . .

Nandini takes the phone, wiping her eyes.

NANDINI. Arun! तुम कहाँ हो . . .? तुम ठीक तो हो . . .?

Ext. Coastal street. Day.

Arun is walking down a street along the ocean in Goa. Palm trees arch overhead. A gentle sea breeze blows under a warm sun.

ARUN. हाँ I'm fine, Nandini . . .

Intercut phone call:

NANDINI. But where in the hell are you? There is no conference in Delhi.

Arun is quiet.

NANDINI. Arun . . . कहाँ हो तुम . . .?

ARUN. जहाँ भी हूँ, ठीक हूँ . . . दो दिन में वापस आ जाऊँगा . . .

NANDINI. Arun . . . why . . . किसलिए . . .? Is there someone else in your life . . .? I Can't believe कि तुम किसी और के लिए मुझे धोखा दे सकते हो . . .?

Arun's eyes are riveted on a couple entering a restaurant across the street: a bent-over, grey-haired man, who uses a walking stick, arm-in-arm with Susanna, now 58. She looks rejuvenated, with shorter hair and a smart, well-tailored suit.

NANDINI. एक है . . . वो जिन्दा है . . .? Arun . . . ? Susanna जिन्दा है . . .?

Arun cuts the call and looks at the sea.

Int. Restaurant. Day.

Susanna shares a table with an older man near the outdoor patio of the restaurant. She calmly takes the older man by the hand.

SUSANNA. I feel such comfort just by looking at you.

The older man smiles.

OLDER MAN. It all comes down to love, sweetheart. और समय चाहिए सोचने के लिए?

SUSANNA. नहीं—सोच लिया . . .

The old man picks his cane and places his hat on his head.

OLDER MAN. ठीक है . . . फिर कल church में 11 बजे . . .

The old fellow pecks Susanna on her cheek. Arun steps aside for him as he leaves the restaurant.
  Unable to suppress a bitter smile, Arun goes to Susanna's table and stands there. Susanna feels his presence but doesn't look up.

SUSANNA. जानती थी एक दिन तुम आओगे . . .

ARUN. आपका उधार चुका दिया . . . इसी जनम में . . . साहेब . . .

Susanna looks at him, and their eyes meet. He is expressionless.

SUSANNA. तुम्हारी साहेब मर चुकी है . . . Sugar . . .

She smiles.
Cut to:

Ext. Goa street. Day.

Arun and Susanna walk in silence down a leafy sun-dappled lane overlooking the beach.

SUSANNA (*voice-over*). मुझे खुद भी अंदाजा नहीं था कि मैं तुम से किस कदर जुड़ी हुई थी . . . तुम्हारे जाने के बाद बस जीने की वजह ढूंढ रही थी . . .

Int. Church. Night.

It rains heavily as Susanna stands in the middle of the church, looking at Jesus with questioning eyes. She takes out a bottle

*of pills, opens it and empties it into her upturned mouth. In
very slow motion, pills fall over her tongue.*

SUSANNA (*voice-over*). फिर एक दिन तुम्हारी शादी की खबर
आई . . . अब इससे अच्छी वजह और क्या मिलती खुदकुशी के लिए . . .
Cut to:

Int. Church. Night.

*Maggie opens the doors of the church to find Susanna lying
unconscious on the floor. As the lightning crackles, we see
foam oozing out of her mouth. Maggie screams.*

MAGGIE. Miss साहेब!

Ext. Road outside Susanna's House. Night.

*Ghalib tries to stop the speeding vehicles on the road amidst
the heavy downpour. When no car stops, he finally stands in
the middle of the road. A car screeches to a halt. The driver
rolls down the window and screams.*

DRIVER. हरामज़ादे मेरी गाड़ी ही मिली तुझे मरने के लिए . . .

Ghalib rushes to him with folded hands.

GHALIB. अस्पताल तक जाना है . . . गाड़ी, phone सब ख़राब हो गये
हैं . . . वहाँ घर में हमारी मेम साहेब मर जाएंगी . . . please खुदा के
लिए . . .

*The driver looks at the passenger seat. The passenger—who
we will later come to know as Dr Tarafdar—a dignified man,
comes into the light and raises his hand like Buddha. A halo
is created around his head from the headlight of the vehicle
behind his car.*
Cut to:

Ext. Susanna's house. Continuous.

Dr Tarafdar walks through the rain down the pathway leading to the church.

Cut to:

Int. Church. Continuous.

Dr Tarafdar checks Susanna's pulse, wearing a stethoscope, while passing on instructions to Maggie and Ghalib.

SUSANNA (*voice-over*). मैं बेसबर थी, उतावली थी, . . . अपने येशू की बाँहों में पहुँचने के लिए . . . पर येशू शायद घबरा गऐ थे . . . last-minute hitch . . . इसलिए उन्होंने अपने एक फरिश्ते को भेज दिया मेरे पास . . .

DR TARAFDAR. साढ़े बारह नींबू बीज अलग . . .तीन अदरक, छोटी छोटी 7 काली मिरी, दो हरी, तीन लाल . . . अलसी का तेल है तो ठीक नहीं तो सरसों का और सबसे ज्यादा important . . . 10 . . . रोशून साबुत . . .

Maggie and Ghalib speak in unison.

MAGGIE. What . . .?

GHALIB. क्या . . .?

Dr Tarafdar tries to remember the Hindi name for 'roshoon'.

DR TARAFDAR. रोशून . . . अरे वो होता है ना white-white छीलते हैं . . . बास आती है बहोत . . .

GHALIB. मूली . . .?

Dr Tarafdar holds his eyebrows, trying hard to remember.

DR TARAFDAR. No . . . white-white . . . That thing . . .

MAGGIE. शलगम . . .?

Dr Tarafdar keeps shaking his head.

GHALIB. चावल!

MAGGIE. चीनी!

GHALIB. चूना!

MAGGIE. Chewing gum.

GHALIB. Ice cream.

MAGGIE. Toothpaste.

Dr Tarafdar screams.

DR TARAFDAR. No!

Ghalib and Maggie look at each other.

GHALIB (*whispers*). Tubelight.

Dr Tarafdar opens his eyes and starts laughing in anger.

DR TARAFDAR. बाह . . .! Tubelight काट के तुम सब्ज़ी में डालता है . . . ईश . . . छातरमाथा . . .

He looks at Susanna and suddenly turns back.

DR TARAFDAR. Garlic . . .

Ghalib shakes his head as Maggie takes a deep breath.

GHALIB. तो लहसुन बोलिए ना . . .

DR TARAFDAR. हाँ हाँ वही . . . और वो bag खोलो वहाँ . . .

He checks Susanna's eyes.

DR TARAFDAR. काँच का एक डब्बे हैं, उसमे से दुई ठो लाल colour के बैंगौर छाता निकालो . . .

Ghalib has opened the bag, turns sharply towards Dr Tarafdar.

GHALIB. छाता . . .?

Dr Tarafdar looks at him through his spectacles on the nose and smiles.

DR TARAFDAR. Mushrooms . . . please . . .

Ghalib takes out two beautiful red-coloured mushrooms from inside the glass jar.
Fade to black.

SUPER—मशरूमदा

Int. Susanna's bedroom. Day.

Susanna is surrounded by Maggie, Ghalib and Dr Tarafdar. All three eagerly wait for her to open her eyes.

SUSANNA'S (*voice-over*). अपनी तरफ से तो मैं मर चुकी थी . . . मगर जब आँख खुली तो कुछ अजीब-सा लगा . . . खुदा की नाक पे नज़र का चश्मा देख कर . . .

Susanna opens her eyes to find Dr Tarafdar looming over her. She moistens her dry lips and whispers.

SUSANNA. कहाँ हूँ मैं . . . इस तरफ या उस तरफ . . .?

DR TARAFDAR. जिस तरफ होना . . . चहिये उस तरफ . . .

SUSANNA. आप . . .?

DR TARAFDAR. Tarafdar . . . Dr Modhushudhon Tarafdar.

Susanna voice over fades in on the soundtrack as Dr Tarafdar smiles.

SUSANNA (*voice-over*). Dr Modhushudan Tarafdar . . . जो बाद में पूरे घर के लिए मोधू दा हो गये थे . . . medical science का अदभुत चमत्कार थे . . .

Cut to:

Int. Kitchen/Solarium. Day.

Susanna's voice-over continues as the camera travels inside the kitchen. The slab is full of ginger, garlic, mushrooms and other vegetables. Dr Tarafdar cuts the vegetables to mix it with some colourful syrup kept in some transparent glass bottles. He finally pours everything into the vessel on the stove and stirs it with the boiling soup inside. He then uses a big serving spoon to fill the bowl to the top with the soup.

SUSANNA (*voice-over*). Allopathy, naturopathy, ayurveda and spirituality का नायाब संगम . . . रहने वाले तो Calcutta के थे मगर उनके नुस्खे पूरी दुनिया में फैले हुए थे . . . New York, Toronto, Sydney, Delhi . . . Madras . . . सब जगह उनके health farm मौजूद थे, दूर दूर से उन्हें medical institutes में lecture के बुलाया जाता था . . . मेरी किस्मत थी की उस रात उन्हें मेरे शहर में होना था . . .

Ext. Solarium. Continuous.

A frail-looking Susanna is seated in a robe, staring obstinately at the soup in the tray. Maggie and Ghalib are smiling at her, hoping that she will have it. Susanna sweeps everything to the floor.

Cut to:

Int. Kitchen. Continuous.

Dr Tarafdar—busy cleaning and putting mushrooms back in their respective jars in the kitchen—reacts to the sound of a tray and glass bowl hitting the floor. He whispers to himself.

DR TARAFDAR. छातरमाथा . . .

Int. Solarium. Continuous.

Dr Tarafdar reaches the solarium, holding his jar of mushrooms. His walk reflects anger. Maggie silently cries and clears the floor as Ghalib looks on. Dr Tarafdar sits next to Susanna. He opens his jar and takes out a red mushroom.

DR TARAFDAR. इसका नाम Jack o' Lantern है . . . बड़े ही काम का है ये बैंगर छाता . . . थोडा खाओ तो दबाई . . . और ज्यादा तो बिष . . .

He holds his jar upside down in front of her eyes and drops all the mushrooms into her lap.

DR TARAFDAR. बुराई ज्यादा में है . . . ये जान लें आप . . . और ज़्यादा कभी ज़्यादा नहीं होता . . . never . . . हमेशा कम ही होता है . . . जिसने कम में जीना सीख लिया उसे कभी कुछ कम नहीं पड़ता ना पैसा ना ज़िंदगी ना शौहरत ना प्यार . . .

He picks up one mushroom and holds it in front of her eyes and asks her in a very loving tone.

DR TARAFDAR. अब soup में कम डालूँ कि ज्यादा . . . hmmm? बैंगर छाता हिंदी मे . . .

He holds his eyebrows to remember the exact word. Susanna's eyes are swelling up with tears. She whispers.

SUSANNA. कुकुरमुत्ता . . .

Dr Tarafdar looks up and smiles.

DR TARAFDAR. Baah . . . कुकुरमुत्ता.

Dr Tarafdar brushes hair gently in a fatherly manner. Susanna howls and hugs him tightly. He smiles more.

Cut to:

Int. Solarium. Later.

Dr Tarafdar feeds her a bowl of soup. She can't take her eyes of him.

SUSANNA (*voice-over*). ऐसे तीमारदार के लिए तो मैं सारी ज़िंदगी बीमार रहने का तैयार थी . . . और रहती भी, मगर मोधू दा ने promise किया . . . वो भी हिंदी में . . .

Int. Solarium. Day.

Another day. Susanna looks healthier now. Dr Tarafdar holds a glass of juice.

DR TARAFDAR. बादा . . .

SUSANNA. बादा नहीं . . . व,व,व . . . वादा . . .

Dr Tarafdar, in full concentration, rolls his lips as he speaks.

DR TARAFDAR. वो-आदा . . .

He tries to feed her the juice but she refuses.

SUSANNA. वो-आदा नहीं, वादा . . .

DR TARAFDAR . . . किया तो . . . कभी नहीं जाऊँगा
वापस . . .

SUSANNA. वापस . . .

She laughs and hugs him tightly. He stands there, holding the glass of juice, and smiles sheepishly.

Montage.

On a garden table in the shade behind Susanna's house, Dr Tarafdar is squeezing an assortment of fresh fruits. He hands a brimming glass of juice to Susanna, who is seated at his side.

In a high-tech gym, Susanna jogs on a treadmill as Dr Tarafdar supervises.

Dr Tarafdar admiringly displays to Susanna the red-coloured Mushrooms he has grown in the backyard of the house.

Susanna is half-naked on a massage table. Dr Tarafdar pours oil on her back and briskly goes to work, his face a picture of stern concentration.

Early morning on the lawns, dressed in robes, Susanna and Dr Tarafdar are seated side by side at a bubbling fountain. Their eyes are closed in serene meditation.

They stand in front of a big old house.

They stand in front of a big house.

Susanna and Tarafdar plant his medicinal plants and mushrooms in the garden of the house.

Tarafdar's cabin is being set up with many books and magazines on health-care and wellness.

Susanna opens a box full of T-Shirts with 'The Art of Dying—Live Healthy and Die Healthy' printed on them. She hands one each to Ghalib and Maggie. Tarafdar looks on with a huge grin on his face.

A dozen guests are gathered at a ribbon-cutting ceremony to inaugurate the doctor's new clinic. They all applaud as a board is placed on the wall outside the house.

SUSANNA (*voice-over*). मोधू दा के पास यूँ तो हर बिमारी के इलाज का नुस्खा था, मगर वो सबसे ज़्यादा मशहूर थे अपने ईजाद किए हुए course के लिए: The Art of Dying—Live Healthy and Die Healthy . . . ज़िंदगी की साझेदारी से पहले हमने पेशे की साझेदारी का फैसला किया—'The Art of Dying' की अपने शहर में branch खोलकर . . .

A Board outside the house announces:
                    Dr Tarafdar's
    'The Art of Dying—Live Healthy and Die Healthy'
Sweating and wheezing, a dozen strangers are jogging around the grounds in expensive athletic wear. Leading them is Susanna, clad in a tracksuit.
    Ghalib is manning the drinks table, handing out frosty glasses of senna pod juice.

SUSANNA (*voice-over*). Massages, enemas, ice-cold showers . . . Everyone loved it . . . The Art of Dying was a hit.

On the patio, Dr Tarafdar administers a deep-tissue massage to a squirming, moaning middle-aged man.
    Maggie carries a sinister-looking rubber bag and water hose as she pursues a nervous old gentlemen across the lawn.
    They exchange a romantic glance while going about their work.

Int. Marriage hall. Day.

Susanna and Dr Tarafdar get married in a traditional Bengali ceremony. People throw flowers on them. As Susanna looks into his eyes lovingly, the flowers turn into mushrooms and fall on the bride and groom.

SUSANNA (*voice-over*). मैं शादी के हक़ में नहीं थी, मगर मोधू दा मुझे अपनी जायदाद का वारिस बनाना चाहते थे . . . उन्हें डर था कि कहीं अगर उन्हें मुझसे पहले कुछ हो गया तो उनकी पहली बीवी और उसकी नालायक बेटी मेरी ज़िंदगी हराम कर देंगे . . .

Int. Susanna's bedroom. Night.

Dr Tarafdar enters the bedroom holding a big mushroom in between his teeth. Susanna comes close, and the lights go off as they start to eat it together.

Ext. Airport. Day.

Susanna waves from outside as Dr Tarafdar enters the airport wheeling his suitcase.

SUSANNA (*voice-over*). मेरी ज़िंदगी तो ज़मीं की ही थी, पर मैं आसमान में उड़ रही थी . . .

Cut to:

Int. Susanna's bedroom. Night.

Susanna's calmly sleeps alone on her bed.

Int. Living room. Same.

A masked man walks stealthily across the living room in the darkness.

Int. Susanna's bedroom. Same.

Susanna opens her eyes as she hears a noise elsewhere in the house.

Int. Living room. Same.

The masked man is hidden behind the curtains. He looks at the shards of the broken lamp that lies on the floor. He takes out a butcher knife. The knifes edge shines in the darkness.

Int. Susanna's bedroom. Same.

The masked man creeps into the bedroom and walks towards

the bed. As he gets closer, Susanna comes out from behind the cupboard, holding an iron rod. She is about to hit him, when he turns. A beat.

He swipes at her with the knife, but she wards off the blow, bringing the iron rod down on to his shoulder—WHAM!

The man goes down on his knees. He groans. Susanna runs out of the room, screaming. The man follows her outside.

Int. Staircase. Same.

She goes down the staircase, and the lights come on. Ghalib enters, holding a loaded rifle. Susanna points upstairs. Ghalib runs up to the living room to find the window open, swinging in the blowing wind.

Ghalib walks to the window and peeps out—everything is still in the darkness as the sound of the crickets fills the air.

Fade out.

Ext. Susanna's house. Day.

Dr Tarafdar pulls up to the house in his Mercedes. As he unloads an overnight bag and laptop case from the front seat, he sees a couple of police cars parked near the garage and some cops standing on the lawn with Susanna.

Ext. Garden. Day.

When she sees her husband coming across the grass, Susanna runs to him and throws her arms around his neck. He holds her tight, stroking her hair as he takes in the broken window and the worried servants.

Int. Bedroom. Night.

Susanna carries a stack of towels to the bathroom door and taps on it with her foot.

The door opens and Dr Tarafdar leans out in a cloud of steam. He's naked and dripping wet. He shoots her a grateful smile as he takes one of the towels and throws it over his head, drying his hair.

In the mirror, Susanna catches sight of his back. A long, ugly bruise is visible on his shoulder! She freezes.

In a moment, her husband is looking at her again and she recovers her composure. But as he shuts the door, there is a trace of worry in his face, too.

SUSANNA (*voice-over*). दुनिया के सारे ग़लत आदमी मेरे ही नसीब में लिक्खे हैं शायद . . .

Cut to:

Int. Bedroom. Later.

Darkness and silence in the master bedroom in the small hours of the morning. The door cracks open as, once more, the burglar is there.

He tiptoes to the bed, raises the butcher knife, then plunges it down!

He stabs again and again until he realizes that the mound under the blankets is not Susanna but a wad of bath towels.

The man peels off his nylon-stocking mask—it's Dr Tarafdar.

SUSANNA (*voice-over*). हालांकि उसे ख़बर थी कि वो अगर मुझसे सच कहता, तो पलक झपकते मैं उसे इस दर्द से छुटकारा दिला देती . . . उसके कर्ज़ से मेरा ख़ज़ाना कम नहीं, होता . . . मगर उसे कम नहीं ज़्यादा चाहिए था . . .

Dr Tarfdar permits himself a grim smile of respect.

Int. Health institute. Night.

All alone in his office, enjoying a glass of Scotch, Dr Tarafdar puts his feet on his desk and leans back, talking—it seems—to no one.

DR TARAFDAR. आर जीग्गेश कोरबे ना दादा . . . सब कर लिया police paper, पूजा . . . अब तो लगता है कि . . .

The camera slowly comes around to reveal the Bluetooth earpiece he is wearing. Phone call continues.

DR TARAFDAR. कि कहीं . . . उसने दोबारा तो ख़ुदकुशी . . . दो हफ़्तों से ज़्यादा हो गए उसे ग़ायब हुए . . .

He gulps his drink down and makes the sound of choking and crying while grinning at himself in the mirror.

DR TARAFDAR. आमी . . .? clinic में हूँ . . . घर नहीं जाया जाता, काटने को दौड़ता है . . . हर चीज़ वहाँ उसकी याद दिलाती है . . . दादा किजो कोरबो माथाये धूकछे ना . . . घीलु खाली

Cut to:

Ext. Susanna's house. Night.

Dr Tarafdar parks his car and walks a bit unsteadily to the front door.

Int. Upstairs corridor. Same.

Approaching the master bedroom Dr Tarafdar spots a fruit basket waiting for him on a hall table. It is exactly the same as the one Susanna sent to Eva. Dr Tarafdar rummages through the fruits and selects an apple. He takes a bite and enters the bedroom.

Int. Bedroom. Continuous.

Dr Tarafdar takes off his clothes while singing a Bengali Rabindra Sangeet song.

DR TARAFDAR. तोमार होलो शुरू अमार होलो शारा . . .

A female voice sings the second line from behind.

FEMALE VOICE. तोमाई अमाई मिले एमनी बोहे धारा . . .

Dr Tarafdar turns sharply to find Susanna standing next to the window.

She looks very attractive in the soft, romantic light of a single lamp. He is shocked to see her but composes himself the next moment.

DR TARAFDAR. कहाँ थी तुम . . .?

Susanna smiles and sings the next line.

SUSANNA. तोमार जोले বাती . . .

Dr Tarafdar walks towards her.

DR TARAFDAR. Why . . .?

SUSANNA. तोमार घोरे साथी . . .

He stands next to her.

DR TARAFDAR. तुम्हारे बिना . . . कहाँ कहाँ नहीं ढूँढा तुम्हें . . .

SUSANNA. तोमार तोरे . . .

She forgets the next word and asks Dr Tarafdar.

SUSANNA. Hmm . . .? तोमार तोरे . . .

Dr Tarafdar sings the word.

DR TARAFDAR. राति . . .

SUSANNA. आमार तोरे . . .

She stops again.

DR TARAFDAR. Tara . . . You don't know how much I missed you, Susanna.

He tries to hug her but she slips away. They both now stand on the two sides of the bed. She takes off her gown while singing.

SUSANNA. तोमार आछे डांगे अमार आछे झोल . . .

She slips into the blanket.

SUSANNA. तोमार बोशे थाका अमार . . .

She looks at Dr Tarafdar with inviting eyes. He turns and takes off his pants.

DR TARAFDAR. चोलाचोल . . .

Dr Tarafdar is about to get into the blanket but suddenly stops. His attention is fixed on some sinuous movement in the sheets. He pulls back the covers, revealing one of Susanna's cobra's, which rises to greet him, it's tongue flicking. Tarafdar utters a strangled cry and staggers back while bundling the snake in the blanket. He then turns and throws the writhing sheet out of the window. He takes a while to get his breath back. A smile slowly emerges on his lips as he turns.

DR TARAFDAR. तोमार हाते रोई अमार हाते खोई . . .

He moves towards her in a serpentine walk, gets on the bed, flicking his tongue like a cobra. he reaches very close to her face and sings softly.

DR TARAFDAR. तोमार मोने भोई आमार भोई हारा . . .

Susanna's face is expressionless. Her eyes are cold—she is in a war now and she knows it.

Cut to:

Int. Kitchen. Day.

Susanna has concealed herself behind the door and is spying on Dr Tarafdar as he prepares a pot of tomato soup. He tosses in a few spices, then speaks without turning around.

DR TARAFDAR. तुम्हारे पीछे vinegar की बोतल रखी है . . . Bring it, please.

Susanna is shocked. She puts on a smile and enters to hand him the bottle. He mixes a few drops from it into the pot.

DR TARAFDAR. मेरी recipe चोरी करना चाहती हो . . .? बोदमाश . . .

He holds out a spoonful of the soup.

DR TARAFDAR. खे दैखो . . .?

SUSANNA. तुमी खे दैखो . . .

Dr Tarafdar slurps up the soup then nods happily.

DR TARAFDAR. बाह . . .!
Cut to:

Ext. Terrace. Day.

Dr Tarafdar emerges from the kitchen, carrying a tray with two bowls of soup. He sets them down on a lazy Susan in the centre of the patio table.
 As Susanna watches intently, he adds some fresh parsley to each one, then rotates the turntable, sending one steaming bowl around to her.
 He smiles encouragingly.
 Instead of eating, she rotates the lazy Susan 180 degrees. Now her bowl of soup is in front of him.

Dr Tarafdar's smile never fades. He sits down, tucks a napkin into his shirt front, and turns the lazy Susan again!

Susanna dreamily inhales the aroma, picks up her spoon and . . . rotates the turntable once more.

Dr Tarafdar's smile has become fierce. He takes the spoonful of soup and, instead of having it himself, offers it to her. She looks him in the eye. He holds the spoon, still smiling at her. A beat.

Suddenly Maggie enters screaming from inside the kitchen.

MAGGIE. Miss साहेब . . . ग़ालिब!

Int. Kitchen. Day.

Inside the kitchen Ghalib lies dead on the floor. Dr Tarafdar bends down to check his pulse. He looks at Susanna and shakes his head. Susanna's eyes turn to the empty bowl of soup lying next to Ghalib's arm.

Cut to:

Ext. Backyard. Day.

Susanna takes out the black plastic sheet from above the rows of mushrooms in the garden. The row sandwiched between the purple and white ones is empty. Her eyes shift to see a single red mushroom lying near the pathway.

Cut to:

Int. Health institute. Day.

Dr Tarafdar is displaying his lab of naturopathy to some of his foreign colleagues. The lab has oversized specimens of garlic, ginger and mushrooms. He turns to see Susanna standing outside the glass window, wearing her black veil costume. His smile fades.

Cut to:

Int. Dr Tarafdar's office. Moments later.

Dr Tarafdar enters his office, where Susanna is waiting for him. She holds up the red mushroom in between her fingers and drops it down on the table.

DR TARAFDAR. Susanna . . . I can explain . . .

WHAM! Susanna slams down one of her father's revolvers on the table. Then she produces a box of bullets and loads one round into the gun. She spins the cylinder, puts the gun to her head and pulls the trigger!
    CLICK!
    WHAM! She slams the gun back on to the desk and glares at Dr Tarafdar. He looks at the gun, as tears start to form in his eyes.

DR TARAFDAR. मुझे पैसों की ज़रूरत थी . . . हर जगेह business में नुकसान हुआ है . . .

Susanna picks up the gun and places it in his shaky palm. A nervous Tarafdar keeps talking.

DR TARAFDAR. Bank loans हैं . . . कई जगह तो warrant भी निकल चुके हैं . . .

He cries and looks at her, begging for mercy.
    Susanna takes the gun from his hand and points it at him. He begins to tremble.

DR TARAFDAR. एक मौका दे दो बस . . . एक मौका . . . मैं तुम्हारी ज़िंदगी से दूर चला जाऊँगा हमेशा-हमेशा के लिए . . .

She pulls the trigger.
    CLICK!
    A cunning smile appears on his lips, as Susanna once again aims the gun at her temple. He eagerly waits for her to pull the trigger. She does . . .

CLICK!
He closes his eyes in despair and starts to cry again.

DR TARAFDAR. I loved you . . . genuinely . . . विश्वास करो मेरा . . . मेरी बेटी की शादी है अगले महीने . . .

Susanna aims the gun back at him again. He shuts his eyes as she pulls the trigger.
CLICK!
He opens his eyes, and a smile slowly appears on his tearful face.
She lifts her eyes, now shining with fury. She turns the gun on him and pulls the trigger four times.
CLICK! CLICK! CLICK! BANG!
The bullet knocks Dr Tarafdar off his feet. He hits the wall, a blotch of blood staining his white medical coat. Grabbing at a lamp, he falls to the floor and dies.

Fade out.

Ext. Road. Night.

Behind the wheel of her car, Susanna makes her getaway on the Panchgani main road. As she rushes towards the farm, two police cars roar by, headed for Tarafdar's wellness centre.

SUSANNA (*voice-over*). क़िस्मत को मेरी आरामदेह मौत गवारा नहीं थी . . . मैं सारी गोलियाँ Tarafdar की लाश के पास छोड़ आई थी . . .

Int. Susanna's house. Night.

The oil portrait of Susanna's father looks down as she enters the dining room, splashing kerosene everywhere.

Int. Foyer. Continuous.

Susanna works her way upstairs, soaking the carpets in kerosene.

Int. Upstairs corridor. Continuous.

She pours the last of the kerosene over the bannister and into the foyer below. She then lights a match and throws it.

A shot in slow motion of the match tumbling down—and igniting the inferno!

Int. Bedroom. Night.

The grandfather clock is ticking. With great dignity, Susanna walks to the rocking chair, and sits in front of the mirror, patiently awaiting the flames to engulf her.

Int. Maggie's quarters. Night.

Maggie, packing her bags, notices something outside. She comes to the window and screams.

From her POV, we see the house engulfed in flames. Already the fire is out of control.

Int. Bedroom. Night.

The room is full of smoke. Coughing and wheezing, Susanna staggers off the chair and tries to open the window. It's jammed.

SUSANNA (*voice-over*). मौत और मुझमें पलक झपकने का फ़ासला बचा था . . . और मुझे अचानक Wasiullah की नज़्म का मिसरा याद आन पड़ा . . . 'साँस लेना भी कैसी आदत है . . . जिए जाना भी क्या रवायत है . . .'

Int. Susanna's house. Night.

The fire is already roaring, bathing the garden in orange light. Maggie comes running and tries to enter the house, fighting her way through the flames.

MAGGIE. Miss साहेब . . .!

Cut to:

Int. Foyer. Moments later.

Maggie starts up the stairway, but the fire makes her step back. A burning beam falls on her, knocking her off her feet. She tries to get up but is pinned to the ground. She screams in pain as the flames burn her skin . . . She looks up towards the corridor.

Int. Bedroom. Continuous.

Susanna finally manages to pry open the window. She can now hear the distant sounds of sirens. Susanna climbs out on to the parapet and jumps down.

Ext. Garden. Night.

Sirens of fire engines blare out loud as they pull up on the drive-way, but its too late. Covered in soot, the other servants watch as the walls of the house collapse.

Ext. Lakeside. Night.

The conflagration is visible across the lake. Flames and flashing police lights are reflected in the dark waves.

Susanna drags herself out of the water, bedraggled and glassy-eyed. She collapses on to the pier and lies there, motionless.

SUSANNA (*voice-over*). मैं अपनी नज़रों में गिर चुकी थी . . . ज़लील हो चुकी थी . . . जिसे तैरना आता हो, उसे कभी डूब के आत्महत्या करने की कोशिश नहीं करनी चाहिए . . .

The camera moves in on Susanna as her head slowly comes up; her eyes are fixed on the distant fire.

Int. Train. Night.

Susanna is sitting on the floor in the general compartment of a crowded moving train. She is shivering inside a dirty, torn blanket. Her clothes are a mess.

She looks ill and starved.

SUSANNA (*voice-over*). अपने कायरपन के लिए खुद को सज़ा दे रही थी मैं . . . हर लम्हा, हर पल, मर कर . . . और फिर मुझे पता चला कि मैं तो मर चुकी हूँ . . .

Susanna notices an old newspaper on the floor, which has her photograph. She picks it up.
    The headline reads—'DNA Samples Confirm Merry Widow's Death'.
    Flashcut: Susanna trying to open the window through the smoke. For a second she turns to hear the faint call of Maggie.

MAGGIE. Miss साहेब . . .!

Cut to:

Int. Private office. Day.

Flashback: Wearing rubber gloves, Arun opens the box and sorts through various bits of cloth and bone, pulling out half a cranium. Then—jackpot!
    He lifts out the skeletal remains of a human foot with six toes.

Int. Train. Night.

Susanna now has tears in her eyes.

SUSANNA (*voice-over*). Maggie का इतना बड़ा बलिदान जाया कर देना पाप होता . . . उसकी कुर्बानी ने एक बार फिर मुझे जीने पे मजबूर कर दिया . . .

Cut to:

Ext. Beach. Dawn.

The present day. Arun and Susanna sit on the rocks behind the house, overlooking the sea. It looks like they've been chatting though the night.

ARUN. मजबूर तो रही हैं आप साहेब . . . सारी ज़िंदगी . . . सारी शादियाँ . . . सारे क़त्ल . . . अपनी हर ज़रूरत को आपने जब चाहा ज़रूरी बना लिया और जब चाहे मजबूरी . . . आपकी दुनिया आपसे शुरू होती है और आप में ही ख़त्म हो जाती है . . . कभी सोचने की ज़हमत की है आपने कि ये गुनाह क्यों किया, आपने . . .? किसके लिए . . .?

Susanna smiles.

SUSANNA. दिल के लिए . . .

Arun laughs.

ARUN. दिल के लिए आपने 6 लोगों को वक़्त से पहले ऊपर भेज दिया . . .

Susanna turns to look at him, a sarcastic smile on her face.

SUSANNA. तुम नहीं समझोगे sugar क्योंकि अब तुम भी एक मर्द बन गए हो . . . तुम लोग सिर्फ़ दिमाग़ से जीना जानते हो और हम लोग बस दिल से जिया करते है . . . और दुनिया की हर बीबी के दिल में कभी न कभी, ये ख़याल आता है, अपने पति से हमेशा हमेशा के लिए छुटकारा पाने का ख़याल . . . अपनी बीबी से पूछ के देखना, उसने भी कोई न कोई तरीक़ा कभी ज़रूर सोचा होगा तुम्हारे क़त्ल का . . .

Arun smiles mockingly, as she continues.

SUSANNA. अपने बचे रहने की वजह जानते हो . . .?

Arun shakes his head.

SUSANNA. तुमने बच्चा दिया है उसे . . . बच्चे के साथ पति को झेलना थोड़ा आसान हो जाता है . . .

ARUN. इसलिए आपने कभी बच्चा पैदा नहीं किया . . .?

Susanna smiles and brushes his hair gently.

SUSANNA. नहीं . . . मेरी वो ज़रूरत शायद तुमसे पूरी होती रही . . . और तुम्हारा प्यार किसी और के साथ न कभी बाँटा था और न ही कभी बाँटूंगी . . .

ARUN. बाँटूंगी . . . ? अब कौन शादी करेगा आपसे . . .? आपकी ख़ूबसूरती अब डरावनी लगने लगी है . . .

Susanna smiles at him.

SUSANNA. ये तो नज़र-नज़र का फ़र्क़ है Sugar. वो मुझे मेरे गुनाहों और बदसूरती के साथ अपना रहा है . . .

Arun looks at her sharply.

ARUN. कौन . . .?

Susanna holds his nose and swings it around gently.

SUSANNA. My seventh husband.

Arun is shocked. Susanna laughs aloud.

SUSANNA. विश्वास नहीं होता . . .

She shows him a church far away across the horizon.

SUSANNA. वहाँ उस church में . . . 11 बजे . . . I am getting married again . . .आओगे ना तुम . . .?

Arun nods.

ARUN. हाँ . . . पर देखने नहीं . . . रोकने . . .

SUSANNA. क्यों . . .?

ARUN. अब किसी और बेगुनाह को मरने नहीं दे सकता . . .

He picks up his jacket and starts to walk away on the beach.
Susanna laughs and calls out to him from behind.

SUSANNA. तुम नहीं बचा सकते हो उसे . . . वो पहले से ही क़ुर्बान हो
चुका है इश्क़ में . . .

Arun keeps walking on the beach. The singing of a choir
fades in on the soundtrack.

Fade to:

Ext. Église de Sacré Coeur de Jesus. Day.

The singing continues as we see the church—a magnificent
Gothic-revival building. In the tower, the bell is ringing. Many
guests are streaming through the main doorway.
    Arun joins them, filled with grim determination.

Int. Église de Sacré Coeur de Jesus. Day.

As the pews are filling up, Arun goes up to the balcony,
where he is alone at the rail. Visibly nervous, he looks down
on the proceedings.

Ceremony.

A choir of Carmelite nuns, clad in brown habits, sings a
Latin hymn as a bride enters, clad in a beautiful, white
wedding gown. Her face is hidden by a white veil. Arun
looks around—something is strange. Where is the groom?
Even more strange: he sees that the bride is not Susanna.
More brides file in, all of them in identical wedding gowns.
Susanna is also there, last in a line of seven! Arun's mouth
is hanging open. The singing stops.
    An elderly bishop steps up to the altar, wearing a surplice
and brocaded chasuble. He's using an ebony cane. Arun
recognizes him as the older man in the restaurant earlier.

An abbot steps forward with a big pair of shears.

Each woman kneels, looking down as the abbot cuts their hair.

Arun grips the rail, fascinated and dismayed by the serene expression on Susanna's face. She looks up as the Bishop walks up to her and slips a gold wedding ring on her finger.

SUSANNA. ये सारा जहां, ये कायनात और इसकी सारी रौनक मेरी रूह को सुकूं नही अता कर सकती क्योंकि सारा सुकूं और सारे सुख मेरे खुदा येशुमसीह से क़ायम है। जो मुझको सबसे प्यारा है। जन्नत का शहनशाह। मै Sister Anna माँ मरियम को साक्षी मानकर अपने प्रभु येशू से ये वादा करती हूँ कि अब मै उसी की बनकर रहूँगी। आज से सिर्फ़ वही एक मेरा मालिक है। मेरा शौहर।

The camera lifts to the balcony—but Arun has left.

Ext. Goa roads. Day.

Nandini and Chetna sit inside a police jeep driving on the roads of Goa. Nandini is glued to the window, trying to look for Arun through the crowd. A bored and uninterested officer accompanies them.

Nandini suddenly notices a man on the other side of the road. His back is facing them. The man turns as he crosses the road.

NANDINI. Arun . . .! गाड़ी रोको please . . . जल्दी!

The jeep swerves to a halt as Nandini jumps out and runs across the road to follow him.

NANDINI. Arun . . .!

Cut to:

Ext. Goa street. Continuous.

Arun stops after a few steps, as he hears somebody call out his name from across the road. He turns to see Nandini standing at the end of the street, panting, trying to catch her breath. He keeps looking at her for a few moments. He is shocked to see her. He walks to her slowly as she runs and hugs him tight, with joyful tears in her eyes.

NANDINI. I hate you, Arun . . . I hate you . . .

Arun embraces her tightly.

ARUN. I am fine, Nandi . . . I told you I'll come back soon.

As he comforts her, he notices Chetna and the cops emerging from across the road. He is alarmed to see them and whispers into Nandini's ear.

ARUN. तुमने क्या बताया है police को . . .?

Nandini looks back at the cops and turns to Arun.

NANDINI. सच नहीं बताया है अभी तक . . . पर अब कभी भी तुमने उससे मिलने की कोशिश की, तो believe me . . . I will kill you . . .

It brings a smile to Arun's face as he hugs her tight.

ARUN. Never . . . She is dead . . .

Nandini looks at him. He wipes her tears.

ARUN. Forever . . . !

NANDINI. चश्मों को क्या हुआ . . .?

ARUNA. नज़र लग गयी . . .
Cut to:

Int. Église de Sacré Coeur de Jesus. Moments later.

The bishop is at the altar, making his concluding remarks. The women in white have exited. But as the singing resumes, they re-enter the nave in single file, all of them now in flowing brown habits. In her new garb, Susanna is unrecognizable. The hymn turns joyful, triumphant. As Susanna kneels and begins to pray, the camera closes in.

Dissolve to:

MONTAGE

Husband #1: The Major, holding his gun, leans over the side of the machaan, eyes wide as the panther races towards him! Susanna is right behind him. With her foot, she shoves him off the platform! He screams as he disappears from view . . .

Husband #2: Jimmy is crawling in the rain, within the graves in the cemetery. Maggie is holding up a syringe and rubber strap, luring him closer . . . He finally snatches the syringe from her hands . . .

Husband #3: Up in the Zabarwan hills overlooking Dal Lake, in the middle of the freezing night, the poet is being buried alive by Goonga, Ghalib and Maggie. Only his head is sticking out, screaming in horror! With their shovels, they heap more and more dirt on to him . . .

Husband #4: As Susanna pulls up the rope ladder, Vronsky screams out to her, in deep passionate longing . . . Suddenly, in the darkness, half a dozen swaying snakes strike . . .

Husband #5: Keemat and Susanna sit in the solarium with drinks in their hands. Susanna is clutching a few Viagra pills. She urges him to take more. Keemat hesitates a few times . . . but then quickly snatches one more and gulps it down . . .

Husband #6: CLICK! CLICK! CLICK! BANG! The bullet knocks Dr Tarafdar off his feet. He hits the wall, a blotch of blood staining his white medical coat. Grabbing at a lamp, he falls to the floor and dies . . .

Int. Église de Sacré Coeur de Jesus. Day.

A shaft of golden sunlight, blazing through the stained glass, singles out Susanna, who's one of the worshippers singing in praise of Jesus. The echoing voices reach the end of the hymn and Susanna lifts her eyes toward the cross on the wall, where Jesus is dying for our sins.

SUSANNA (*singing*) . . . Amen!

Fade out.

Int. Confession box. Day.

The curtain slides open. Through the carved wooden partition, we see Susanna in her habit.

SUSANNA. मुझे अपने गुनाह क़ुबूल करने हैं Father . . . सातों गुनाह . . .

THE END

APPENDIX

susanna's seven husbands

The original short story by
Ruskin Bond

Locally the tomb was known as 'the grave of the seven times married one'. You'd be forgiven for thinking it was Bluebeard's grave; he was reputed to have killed several wives in turn because they showed undue curiosity about a locked room. But this was the tomb of Susanna Anna-Maria Yeates, and the inscription (most of it in Latin) stated that she was mourned by all who had benefited from her generosity, her beneficiaries having included various schools, orphanages and the church across the road. There was no sign of any other grave in the vicinity and presumably her husbands had been interred in the old Rajpur graveyard, below the Delhi Ridge.

I was still in my teens when I first saw the ruins of what had once been a spacious and handsome mansion. Desolate and silent, its well-laid paths were overgrown with weeds, and its flower beds had disappeared under a growth of thorny jungle. The two-storeyed house had looked across the Grand Trunk Road. Now abandoned, feared and shunned, it stood encircled in mystery, reputedly the home of evil spirits.

Outside the gate, along the Grand Trunk Road, thousands of vehicles sped by—cars, trucks, buses, tractors, bullock carts—but few noticed the old mansion or its mausoleum, set back as they were from the main road, hidden by mango, neem and pipal trees. One old and massive pipal tree grew out of the ruins of the house, strangling it much as its owner was said to have strangled one of her dispensable paramours.

As a much-married person with a quaint habit of disposing of her husbands whenever she tired of them, Susanna's malignant spirit was said to haunt the deserted garden. I had examined the tomb, I had gazed upon the ruins, I had scrambled through shrubbery and overgrown rose bushes, but I had not encountered the spirit of this mysterious woman. Perhaps, at the time, I was too pure and innocent to be targeted by malignant spirits. For malignant she must have been, if the stories about her were true.

The vaults of the ruined mansion were rumoured to contain a buried treasure—the amassed wealth of the lady Susanna. But no one dared go down there, for the vaults were said to be occupied by a family of cobras, traditional guardians of buried treasure. Had she really been a woman of great wealth, and could treasure still be buried there? I put these questions to Naushad, the furniture maker, who had lived in the vicinity all his life, and whose father had made the furniture and fittings for this and other great houses in Old Delhi.

'Lady Susanna, as she was known, was much sought after for her wealth,' recalled Naushad. 'She was no miser, either. She spent freely, reigning in state in her palatial home, with many horses and carriages at her disposal. Every evening she rode through the Roshanara Gardens, the cynosure of all eyes, for she was beautiful as well as wealthy. Yes, all men sought her favours, and she could choose from the best of them. Many were fortune hunters. She did not discourage them. Some found favour for a time, but she soon tired of them. None of her husbands enjoyed her wealth for very long!

'Today no one enters those ruins, where once there was mirth and laughter. She was a zamindari lady, the owner of much land, and she administered her estate with a strong hand. She was kind if rents were paid when they fell due, but terrible if someone failed to pay.

'Well, over fifty years have gone by since she was laid to rest, but still men speak of her with awe. Her spirit is restless, and it is said that she often visits the scenes of her former splendour. She has been seen walking through this gate, or riding in the gardens, or driving in her phaeton down the Rajpur road.'

'And what happened to all those husbands?' I asked.

'Most of them died mysterious deaths. Even the doctors were baffled. Tomkins-sahib drank too much. The lady soon tired of him. A drunken husband is a burdensome creature, she was heard to say. He would eventually have drunk himself to death, but she was an impatient woman and was anxious to replace him. You see those datura bushes growing wild in the grounds? They have always done well here.'

'Belladonna?' I suggested.

'That's right, huzoor. Introduced in the whisky-soda, it put him to sleep forever.'

'She was quite humane in her way.'

'Oh, very humane, sir. She hated to see anyone suffer. One sahib, I don't know his name, drowned in the tank behind the house, where the water lilies grew. But she made sure he was half-dead before he fell in. She had large, powerful hands, they said.'

'Why did she bother to marry them? Couldn't she just have had men friends?'

'Not in those days, huzoor. Respectable society would not have tolerated it. Neither in India nor in the West would it have been permitted.'

'She was born out of her time,' I remarked.

'True, sir. And remember, most of them were fortune hunters. So we need not waste too much pity on them.'

'She did not waste any.'

'She was without pity. Especially when she found out what they were really after. Snakes had a better chance of survival.'

'How did the other husbands take their leave of this world?'

'Well, the Colonel-sahib shot himself while cleaning his rifle. Purely an accident, huzoor. Although some say she had loaded his gun without his knowledge. Such was her reputation by now that she was suspected even when innocent. But she bought her way out of trouble. It was easy enough, if you were wealthy.'

'And the fourth husband?'

'Oh, he died a natural death. There was a cholera epidemic that year, and he was carried off by the haija. Although, again, there were some who said that a good dose of arsenic produced the same symptoms! Anyway, it was cholera on the death certificate. And the doctor who signed it was the next to marry her.'

'Being a doctor, he was probably quite careful about what he ate and drank.'

'He lasted about a year.'

'What happened?'

'He was bitten by a cobra.'

'Well, that was just bad luck, wasn't it? You could hardly blame it on Susanna.'

'No, huzoor, but the cobra was in his bedroom. It was coiled around the bedpost. And when he undressed for the night, it struck! He was dead when Susanna came into the room an hour later. She had a way with snakes. She did not harm them and they never attacked her.'

'And there were no antidotes in those days. Exit the doctor. Who was the sixth husband?'

'A handsome man. An indigo planter. He had gone bankrupt when the indigo trade came to an end. He was hoping to recover his fortune with the good lady's help. But our Lady Susanna, she did not believe in sharing her fortune with anyone.'

'How did she remove the indigo planter?'

'It was said that she lavished strong drink upon him, and when he lay helpless, she assisted him on the road we all have to take by pouring molten lead in his ears.'

'A painless death, I'm told.'

'But a terrible price to pay, huzoor, simply because one is no longer needed . . .'

We walked along the dusty highway, enjoying the evening breeze, and some time later we entered the Roshanara Gardens, in those days Delhi's most popular and fashionable meeting place.

'You have told me how six of her husbands died, Naushad. I thought there were seven?'

'Ah, the seventh was a gallant young magistrate who perished right here, huzoor. They were driving through the park after dark when the lady's carriage was attacked by brigands. In defending her, the young man received a fatal sword wound.'

'Not the lady's fault, Naushad.'

'No, huzoor. But he was a magistrate, remember, and the assailants, one of whose relatives had been convicted by him, were out for revenge. Oddly enough, though, two of the men were given employment by the lady Susanna at a later date. You may draw your own conclusions.'

'And were there others?'

'Not husbands. But an adventurer, a soldier of fortune came along. He found her treasure, they say. And he lies buried with it, in the cellars of the ruined house. His bones lie scattered there, among gold and silver and precious jewels. The cobras guard them still! But how he perished was a mystery, and remains so till this day.'

'And Susanna? What happened to her?'

'She lived to a ripe old age. If she paid for her crimes, it wasn't in this life! She had no children, but she started an orphanage and gave generously to the poor and to various schools and institutions, including a home for widows. She died peacefully in her sleep.'

'A merry widow,' I remarked. 'The Black Widow spider!'

Don't go looking for Susanna's tomb. It vanished some years ago, along with the ruins of her mansion. A smart new housing estate has come up on the site, but not before several workmen and a contractor succumbed to snake bite! Occasionally, residents complain of a malignant ghost in their midst, who is given to flagging down cars, especially those driven by single men. There have also been one or two mysterious disappearances.

And after dusk, an old-fashioned horse and carriage can sometimes be seen driving through the Roshanara Gardens. If you chance upon it, ignore it, my friend. Don't stop to answer any questions from the beautiful fair lady who smiles at you from behind lace curtains. She's still looking for an ideal husband.

RUSKIN BOND

Read more in Penguin

DUST ON THE MOUNTAIN: COLLECTED STORIES
Ruskin Bond

'A writer who has, with intense depth and sensitivity, absorbed the essence of the culturally syncretic Indian society'—*Telegraph*

Ruskin Bond wrote his first short story, 'Untouchable', at the age of sixteen in 1950. Since then he has written over a hundred stories, including the classics 'A Face in the Dark', 'The Kitemaker', 'The Tunnel', 'The Room of Many Colours', 'Dust on the Mountain' and 'Time Stops at Shamli'.

Comprising an exhaustive selection from six decades of short fiction by India's best-loved contemporary author, this volume brings together the some of Bond's best short stories.

'[Ruskin Bond's stories] bring to life the special flavours of life in the hills . . . strengthen[s] the "Rudyardian thesis" that [if] the smell of the Himalayas . . . creeps into the blood of a man, he will return to the hills again and again and will love to live and die among them'—*Tribune*

Fiction Omnibus
Rs 499